Crossing-Over: Shade Ops

Paradox F.

Crossing-Over: Shade Ops

This book is a work of fiction. Names, characters, places and incidents are the product of the author's imagination or are used fictitiously. Any resemblance to actual events, locales, or persona, living or dead, is coincidental.

Cover designed by Elisa2B (Janollari)

Swift Studios
1817 Sherwood Forest Circle
League City, TX 77573
swiftstudios@yahoo.com
www.co-comic.com

FIRST EDITION

ISBN: 0-9974891-2-5

Printed in the United States of America

Contents:

Prologue

To the honored Hitoshi clan head,

I hope that things are going well for you back home. This country is so much different than Nihon. First off, Pennotia is its name, and it contains wondrous technology that I have never seen in our lands. Living here takes some time to get used to; I'm still getting used to their way of life. Tall buildings are commonplace, and their streets are filled with automobiles.

I managed to recruit a native ferret, Michael, to aid me. He secured my passage across the seas, which was a lengthy voyage. Apparently, I have to keep my weapons hidden here, but the people here seem friendly enough. Though, it seems like the populace is oblivious to the problems around them. Similar to our society in a way, actually...

Faucet City is where I am currently residing in along with my new help. Their culture takes time to get accustomed to. The air around this place is more informal. I don't mind the freedom, but it can be quite frustrating sometimes when others around become a little too loud. 'Mike' told me to keep silent in these instances. There's no need for me to get arrested for petty disturbances such as that. Eventually, when I get back into my flat, I become exhausted, so I spend my evenings catching up on lost sleep.

It was not long until I convinced Mike to show me around the town shortly after I had settled in. Honestly, there is not much scenery to view unless you go to one of the parks there or the outskirts of the city. What I found intriguing are phones, which are used to talk to people over a distance. Had you possessed one of these devices, I would not need to write you this letter! Resting on their soft mattresses is most comfortable and surely beats lying down on the forest floor, but I still enjoy the outdoors. At least there, I could see the stars. Here, the lights from the fixtures and buildings are so bright that they blot out the beautiful night sky. I definitely miss seeing that.

Anyway, Mike told me to purchase some clothes to blend in better, which I did. It was indeed annoying to go through the trouble of exchanging currency, but I finally obtained new attire. They are slightly tight and cling to my body moreso than the *yukatas* that I'm used to. Of course, you should try the clothes first inside of a changing room to make sure that they fit. It's only common sense.

The food they have here is also amazing, but that's a letter for another day. I haven't forgotten about my mission. The ever-looming threat of the Dark One persists. My investigation into the matter continues and the fate of the world depends on how well I perform my clan duties.

Most of the preferred weapons in their stores are guns like what Tekiya used. While I do appreciate their craftsmanship, those are not the kinds of arms that I'm looking for. There was an assortment of knives at the counters—the customization options were quite excessive. In the end, I had my associate pick some for me, and I told him that I would prefer to use traditional weaponry, unless necessary. He sighed at this for some reason…

Given the situation, I had Mike give me a rundown on anything I may need to know during my stay here. The amount of information was staggering, and before I knew it, the sun was already setting. I plan to meet up with him again first thing in the morning, but I just had to write to you. Hopefully, we can find a lead based on the foreign company that we researched about, the one that Tekiya was managing before the two of us faced off against him.

As I organize my belongings, you should know that I think about our clans and homeland often. Such evil must not be allowed to run amok. Still, it is hard to believe that technology of this level had been in existence around the world since our grandparents' time. I shudder when imagining that Nihon would gradually become as alien as this land.

I do hope that you will write back soon. I worry often enough, so you should tell me as much as you possibly can about everything that I have missed, okay? May your new role continues to flourish, and I hope everyone else back home is doing fine as well. Seriously though, you better reply back, or else...

Your Friend,

Hachi Takaro

CHAPTER 1

Strange Customs

The first few days helped to normalize Hachi to her new surroundings. Ambient noise was something the ferret girl had yet grown accustomed to; her eyes shot red from lack of sleep. Making matters worse, the apartment Michael had acquired for her was the stark opposite of everything she had come to expect from her living quarters. It was a small space where she could barely swing her legs without bumping at a wall, and it was located next to a major thoroughfare that seemed nearly packed with traffic constantly. The noise from the traffic offered no peace, or any chance at all for meditation. It was a vivid contrast to the welcoming chirping of nature that had mostly defined her days of the past. The change was not pleasant, but she had no choice. Adaptation was key as need when it was also part of her training.

Michael had smartly remarked to her that the rent had suffered for that, but once again the shinobi was out of her element, unaware of how economics worked around here. She could not relate to how one could pay for such an excuse of comfort. This was merely a safe haven, somewhere to tuck away while she plans for and executes her mission. What she did know was that her privacy had fled the moment she had set foot on shore.

She stared out at the small window overlooking the evening rush hour, a favorite hobby she had picked up recently. Sitting crossed-legged on her single bed, she surveyed those below. She made a note of their style of dress; how they walked, and their body language, mannerisms that she would have to train herself in like any martial art. Tidbits that she must learn if she were blend in this new world. It had been quite humid, and the storm front finally broke over the city about an hour ago. Like flowers under the sun's first rays, people opened umbrellas in the streets.

Consequently, her viewing was briefly interrupted. It was only in the intersections that she lazily fought against sleep to observe. There was a nagging feeling inside of her, a desire to run out into an open field, which she had yet to satisfy. Under Michael's advice, she stayed indoors, acclimating.

Hachi flipped the blinds closed, clutching the pillow as she fell backward.

I need something to do, she protested internally.

The "television," a black square pushed against the wall, stared at her like a dark, vacant eye. She had only used it once when her new friend and contact first set it up. He had been so enthusiastic about it, clattering off about its benefits as he hooked it all up. She could only watch him with a dull look. Perhaps that's just how folks like him were in this fast-paced, noisy world of theirs.

"It's great, you'll love it," he had said, wholeheartedly believing the magical world beyond it would keep her entertained. In fact, she had not loved it one bit. Instead, she quickly jammed the power button as soon as he had left the premises. It only reminded her of the outside freedoms denied to her, on top of being a pointless distraction. None of the channels within the boxed contraption was alluring nor intriguing to her.

An insect-like buzz snapped Hachi out of her daze. Dancing on the desk, the "pager" or whatever he had called it, spun a lazy circle on the polished wood. A message from the small dull screen of the pager reading, "Meet me downstairs by the front desk, M" scrolled past her. Quick on the draw, Hachi slipped into one of the outfits the male ferret had bought for her. Like the others items Mike had brought her, it felt odd too. The shoes were too stiff and high in the back, so she replaced them with her flat-soled sandals. She wondered how anyone could move swiftly in them. Indifferent to getting them damaged in the rain, she slipped a knife inside a belt within her upper sleeve as she left.

Michael clipped the device back on his person and waited, eyeing the stairs anxiously. The girl was naive around modern conveniences, but she had learned quickly. She reminded him of his ex, the first encounter excluded. He reflexively touched the spot on his neck where Hachi nicked him. It wasn't serious, but still, there was no denying that she had unduly roped him into a huge conspiracy.

It was not that he gave in too early, or even easily. It was when she eased her hold on him that he realized that she had no intentions to kill him. The kunoichi just needed him to do something for her. It had been easy from there on—easy and absurd. He had agreed to her terms, not that he had any choice not to.

He still couldn't figure out what she exactly was, and she wasn't keen on sharing too many details. She was too dumb to be a mercenary but far smarter than a mere street thug. She was something in between, clearly different. Not an ordinary nuisance, she was driven. As far as he could tell, she was acting on her own, or at least with a great deal more independence than one would expect. Perhaps she was a criminal enforcer cutting out some bad blood overseas, or maybe just a killing machine with some screws loose. The fact remained that he was stuck with her for the moment. She liked him enough, so he doubted she would kill him off after she got what she wanted, assuming he kept his head down. No doubt she didn't appear to be the type to be messed with. Liking him or not, he had decided against taking any undue risks. There is that intimidating aura about her that affirmed his instincts.

Finally, Hachi strolled out of the stairwell, breaking him out of his contemplation. He sighed in relief as he noted that she had taken his advice on the clothes, for the most part. The ninja's obstinacy was still apparent, as his eyes trailed her soggy footwear. She's in charge after all, so such matters would be to her loss, not his.

"Where are we going?" she asked, absently brushing down a cowlick.

"For coffee," he said simply. Hachi was always the type to be direct, when it comes to him. He had nothing against it. Together, they left the lobby and waded into the mob, beating against the tide until they came within sight of a flashing neon sign showing a repeating series of frames, a mug being forever stirred by a spoon. Inside the café, the bustling noise of the city was replaced by the sound of flatware on porcelain and the murmur of dinner conversation. Yet, the humming was a marginal improvement from the ferret girl's apartment.

"Find us a seat. I have to call a waitress over." Hachi let her shoulders relax, suddenly realizing how anxious she had been. She felt like the large crowd could hide any number of hunters or spies out for her blood. There they were, all at tables conversing, with one or two loners sitting by themselves. Any one of them might be under a disguise. Inside though, the coffeehouse patrons were absorbed in their own lives. They paid her no attention as they chit-chatted amongst themselves, read newspapers, or wrote notes.

Hachi scanned around, spotting an empty booth near the back corner. From there, she had a clear view of the entire establishment and the safety of a wall at her back. Slipping off her raincoat, she peered around to see where her companion had gone. With preciseness, she swept around the whole café interior in just a single glance, taking in the position of everyone and whatever their attention may be on. Mike was leaning on the checkout counter making small talk to a scrawny hen fiddling with receipts. She laughed as he finished up and walked towards his table, smiling all the way.

"What are you up to?"

Sitting beside her in their booth, he kept his grin. "Oh, nothing really. I'm a bit of a regular here, you see, and I was the one who actually referred that gal for the job. I was just catching up, seeing how she was doing."

The ferret girl studied his face as he spoke. Sure that he was being honest, she let her shoulders slump again. Michael wondered at how easily she change demeanor. One minute, she was on edge, ready to spring up and down. Next, she switched to a more relaxed countenance. "I had something to talk to you about. I went digging after you mentioned that particular name to me earlier and I think I found some answers, but I need to know something right here and now before I tell you."

"You brought me here to have witnesses," she remarked. He gave a brief pause, nervous of her presence. That was odd of him, she thought. He had been friendly the whole way here.

"What are you here for? You're not a tourist, and don't tell me anything else other than your reason. I'm in enough trouble if I

8

guessed right." He believed that he had a right to know. If he was going to stick his neck further into her mess, she better let him know what's up. He was not about to be running around like a headless friller.

The young Takaro sighed and gave him a brief explanation of her mission with what little details she could spare. Though Mike was hesitant at first to stick around, she dissuaded him from leaving by flashing one of her hidden blades. She hated to do that to him but she needed him to stay, and she can't trust him with every detail. She recounted her tale of assassination and revenge, all the way up to her interrogation of the hyena, Tekiya. "I came here to stop this Dark One, a force he claimed was capable enough to destroy the world. I need your information in order to hunt him and his minions down."

Mike was silent throughout her tale, simply taking it all in with a slightly incredulous look on his face. When she finished speaking, he exhaled deeply, craning his head backward.

"So what? You're like, a ninja or something?" Hachi only chuckled at that. "This is way over my head, Hachi. I can't go assassinating people like this with you. I have a handsome head that I want to keep on my shoulders." His voice dropped to a whisper as he continued, "Lockhardt has power. A lot of it, and he won't just roll over with what little I could collect. You're asking me to join you in this, whether you meant it or not."

Hachi considered that last statement for a second. It never dawned on her that Mike was a businessman. He mentioned it before, but the fact had fallen out the other ear just as quickly. Until now, he was nothing more than another informant to her, a piece of the puzzle to get her closer to her mark. She felt embarrassed for putting him in this situation, even though it was the only method she knew how. The shinobi recalled how their first scene played out. I threatened him into bringing me here. I made him care for me, and do the dirty work all while I was kept safe.

"I--I'm sorry. I didn't think about it." Mike caught the attention of a server. He ordered a carafe and fresh cream. "If you want to leave…" she left the word hanging, knowing he would figure out the rest.

Mike looked back at Hachi. She saw that his expression was resigned, accepting this turn of events. It crushed a tiny part of her to have used him like this. "It's too late now, Hachi. I already dipped my fingers in this." He poured out the coffee for both of them; it smelled slightly of the chemical cleaner that Hachi had watched some custodians using down her apartment hallway once. It tasted bitter, like reheated water mixed with salt and soap.

"That name you gave me, Tekiya, it didn't come up on any public records. I spent some time searching for him though; I knew you were from that island and probably, so was he. I had a favor pulled, and after a lot of funds were pushed under the table--" he gave her a sidelong glance "--somebody gave me the name Lockhardt. It turns out he's the brother to your Tekiya as far as we know, probably the bankroll of his operations. He owns a big chunk of the cash flow where he works."

"Who is he exactly?" Hachi gripped her mug tightly, excited at this fresh news. The caffeine wasn't helping matters either.

"An invisible hand. He manipulates the weapon markets through his corporate board so that he has leverage in every major competitor's pots. He's pretty much untouchable to anyone coming off the streets." He left the explanation in the air. The amount of security for someone that powerful would be enormous, and getting to him would pose a number of challenges which Hachi had never faced before in this land. "He's almost never alone, and he likes his high rise skyscrapers."

"So how do you suggest I get to him?" Hachi asked. Before Mike could answer, her attention was drawn by another patron a few tables down folding up a newspaper. She was reptilian, doubled up against the cool air with a tan sweater showing under an overcoat she hadn't bothered to remove. Her slatted eyes gazed at Mike knowingly, and Hachi could sense that this was a setup. The ferret girl made a mental note for this sort of encounter, the urban landscape left a lot to an assumption, and she wanted to be better prepared for surprises. Without a cue, the lizard seated herself in the ferrets' booth holding her own mug.

Mike introduced her as Nicoletta Dency, a receptionist for one of the higher-ups where he obtained his intel. She lounged, taking up as much free space as she could in a self-important manner like it was a privilege just to be in her presence. So much for being a receptionist.

"I can get you in close at a business meeting." Her way of talking made Hachi's skin crawl. "There's going to be a video conference tomorrow; their brokers are negotiating to split the company through contract agreements. Mr. Lockhardt is supposed to be sitting in as final spokesperson when they close the deal so I imagine you can gather some information on him indirectly."

Hachi didn't approve of this kind of runaround. Her experience had always been in eliminating targets in person, not the kind of espionage that the lizard had proposed. "What do I do?" The ninja asked, burying deep her anxiety. Dency leered through the steam of her second refill, a faint glow amidst a fog like a spirit guarding a bridge.

"You do nothing but what I tell you."

"Dency," Mike piped up, noticing tension growing between the two ladies. "You were paid to do this, so stop being a smartass. Hachi needs to get to him in person, any ideas?"

Undeterred, the green reptile scoffed. "This isn't a game," she replied through grit teeth. He bumped Hachi's shoulder in annoyance cutting off the retort she had in mind.

"Dearie, if you want my help then you must do things my way. If you're not willing to play by my rules, then I will take the down payment and leave." The table fell silent which prompted the insider to continue. "Alright," she hissed knotting her fingers together. "I have free space in a maintenance company hired for your target's building. Luckily for you, they are scheduled to do a check-up of the duct systems on the center floor. That would be our entrance ticket."

****

Hachi adjusted her footing above the central grate. Striated light gave her eyes enough to work with, though she could not see anything that wasn't directly below her. Her task was to eavesdrop, and the sheet metal made every noise echo quite well including her breathing. Going by her watch, it had been three hours since Nicoletta's crew had left her here. She had to give that cold-blooded woman credit. Dency knew exactly where Hachi would need to be in order to eavesdrop out undetected, and had meticulously planned every aspect of the operation ahead of time. Who was she? The ferret knew this went deeper than just the lure of Mike's bribe and hoped that he knows to be careful when dealing with individuals such as her.

Her attention was drawn to a keycard scanner beeping outside. There was a click, then a drag of the wooden door over a doormat. She held herself back and leaned forward ever so slightly to see an unassuming terrier in a black suit. He had his hair combed at the middle and swept back in an odd style that made it looked mismatched. This canine had to be the company spokesperson, Hachi mused. She could make out the shuffling of drawers and some tapping on a keyboard. Those sounds were alien to her a week ago, yet so much had changed.

Underneath her in the office, the terrier was dialing a phone call. The young ninja tensed expectantly.

"Carol, call him in." The dog dictated onto the phone. A short time later, someone else Hachi couldn't properly see wheeled something into the office. He left as soon as he entered, so it wasn't anyone important. The ninja girl squinted hard, creating as much space as she could to lean more closer, without making as much as a single decibel of noise. The terrier came back underneath the vent holding a black plastic rectangle. A click followed with some whirrs and then a new voice was speaking inside the room. There were no footsteps, so that spokesman must have not yet returned to his desk. She needed to see what he was doing. How could a meeting occur when she heard no one else coming to the office?

Loosening her muscles a bit, she made her move. The oil on her shoes suppressed the regular screeching sound, though it did mean she had to rely on the weak spots of construction for support. As she descended closer, the voices died off to be replaced by a shuffling of numerous chairs. Now her curiosity was piqued. From what she had seen, the room below lacked the

14

space to accommodate such numbers. Hachi stopped half a meter from the surface, now able to see a substantial portion of the suite much better. Indeed, the terrier was standing by the cart, tuned to television much larger than the one at her quarters. A long meeting table stretched out from its picture, some thirty individuals quietly setting into their own seats. Hachi scanned their faces, but the distortion was too much from this angle, and she could not see anyone resembling her target.

Hachi briefly marveled at the wonders of this new world. Here's an individual having a meeting with others from a television. Perhaps it was their way of being inconspicuous—a means of being somewhere without being physically present. Whatever the case, the ferret would worry about that later. She only to gather enough intel to locate Lockhardt from the task the haughty lizard had sent her on.

The first topic of note discussed by the executives was the closure of a company called Securihans. Some of the terms discussed may have been exotic, but she could add up the numbered graphs and understand through the terms that Mr. Lockhardt had come out on top out of this deal. The terrier was to be "downsized," though he seemed unconcerned about this, barely even reacting. He seemed to act stoic and unyielding, despite the overwhelming amount of financial dealings being discussed. Hachi glazed over as the recording dragged on, still wary but not paying as much attention to the drivel coming out of that screen. Not until she heard the meeting begin to wrap up did she perk up again.

"Our benefactor would like to conclude this meeting personally. Please wait while we bring him up." The television darkened for a few moments, the walls having jumped to a much smaller office room. A single lamp off-screen burned a bright white in the darkness, only able to accent the large desk and a hand holding what looked to be a pen.

"My condolences for your misfortune," came a voice from the veiled figure. He had a quiet voice, neither nasal nor feminine. "I understand you are not going to be part of our merger. It saddens me to hear this, so I invite you to attend my shareholder's party this coming Goodrei to discuss an alternative position." The shadowy figure made some unseen gestures in the dark background before moving his pen to write something. Then, he raised a scrap of paper to the camera like a used napkin. Hachi leaned forward further to try to see the note at a proper angle. She could only decipher one word of the stylized note before it was lowered back down.

"Come at ten o'clock. Don't be late." The ferret heard the tone as a command from a superior and so did the spokesman below, judging from the way he shuddered. The tape ended in static, which signaled her cue to exit. She pulled her arms back over her head, positioning her legs carefully until she was lying flat on her stomach. Then, she squirmed back towards the vent opening, considering her next move.

****

The terrier, unaware of the intruder, flopped heavily back into the leathery chair. The recording of the tape still played out the empty static remainder in its reel, clouding his thoughts somewhat. Securihans was now broke, thanks to a suspicious financial advisor, brought on by Lockhardt himself years ago, who had poured more than half of their market value in dummy stocks, which irreparably ruined their capital. When they

16

declared bankruptcy, his assets evaporated, and of course, the insurance agency couldn't keep up with insider information, so his best course of action was to hold a vote to dismantle the operation. He rubbed his eyes. The party meeting was hardly an offer that he could refuse. His hand was forced, he had to go or become destitute.

He ejected the videotape in resignation. For a fleeting moment, he longed to smash that blasted tape under his foot. But that passed as quick as it came, and he left his door to call in sick. His career was already forfeit anyway. Perhaps a short vacation would do him good.

CHAPTER 2

Of Interest

A cold front had blown the storm over, sending chilly rain that quickly dropped the night's temperatures. The city now held a dreariness more poignant than before. Residents bundled in extra layers, conversations on the street were brief if not absent. The air was misty, and the few people out in the street could be seen blowing heat. It was a sign of a season coming to a close.

Mike slipped his acquisition paperwork into the manager's slot next to his office. The sound of its soft landing barely registered as it hit the back wall of the other side. It was nearly supper, and he wanted to clock out of work earlier. He had plans made prior by phone to catch up with Hachi, wondering what she was planning next. It's still difficult to tell whatever goes on in her head but he was slowly learning. Work had kept his schedule busy for a few days since their time at the diner.

The calls she had made since then incessantly informed him how uncomfortable she was with modern conveniences. The Takaro cringes from the mere mention of tech and thinks that her orthodox methods as best. At this, the male ferret firmly shot down the notion of her visiting him at his job. The last thing he needed was to deal with her inexperience around his colleagues, who were too wound up in their upper-class social circles to know anybody making less than six figures. But as much as he feared for his life and his job, Hachi admittedly gave him a thrill of excitement that he never knew he was missing. Something he couldn't quite describe perfectly but he found it to be quite interesting. Much like a childhood adventure fantasy, except dangerously real. Saying goodbye to his co-workers to kill the little time left on the clock, he waved off-handedly back to the front door and flipped his collar up, smiling slightly.

Before he had gotten off of the crosswalk a block away, he felt a hand upon his shoulder. It was large and heavy. "Come back for another?" A voice spoke to his left ear. He recognized it and immediately knew what was about to happen. He needn't look back. He knew better than to act funny. He merely suppressed his initial panic and shrugged on like nothing was amiss.

"How's the weather up there?" Mike asked, trying to keep his voice steady.

"Good, good. My feathers catch dirt like crazy, but I do like the fall."

Mike, without looking back, walked into a parked green van nearby away from the rush hour traffic. Another thug, donning grey overalls with black boots and a baseball cap exited the passenger side and opened the rear doors. The salaryman climbed in, nestled between two piles of mechanical hardware.

"Hey," he said to no one in particular, trying to make small talks to calm his racing pulse. Somehow, he was apprehensive of what was to come. Rather than a reply, he merely found a sharp pain on his arm. Even before he could register a yell, he felt himself tiring out. The last thing his eyes saw before a wave of darkness crept over him, was the door of the van rushing shut as the vehicle begins to zoom off at normal speed like nothing happened.

Next time he came to, Mike found himself sitting in a chair at an isolated room. Crates littered the room here and there, and nauseating darkness was light dimly by a small bulb hanging by a black wire, hissing above his head as it burned. He was tied to a chair in the middle of the untidy industrial warehouse devoid of windows—not like the excuse of a hole that ripped the concrete side walls at the top and covered with small louvers can pass for a window. His chair felt slightly damp from water dripping out of a nearby cracked wall. From the corner of his eye, he spotted a pipe dripping from a junction weld. The walls were bare concrete, old and telling the sign of use. Opposite of him was a rusted steel door to the abandoned industrial warehouse, which he currently occupied. The only door it seemed, for as far as his eyes could see, there were no others.

Not like it was his first time. In order to stay useful to Hachi, he had to dip his mitts into shady waters. A trade secret or two, and a few monetary bribes. He was in deep, and his window of escape from this skullduggery was closing fast.

A new lackey poked his head in, before signaling behind him after seeing Mike awake. "Coming in!" He called out. Through the door stepped a blue gecko, who tipped his hat to greet him.

"Hullo, Charles," Mike said, stretching his legs.

"Hello, Michael. Had a nice drive?"

"Fine enough."

"Great to hear," the reptile smiled. A rolling chair followed behind him after the stallion guard brought it in. "Now," Charles began, "I have word that Nicoletta met a friend of yours earlier this week. She tells us you had a big favor to ask."

"I paid her in full." The ferret promptly answered.

The cold-blooded host shook his head. "Not important. By the way, we're not upset over any of this, so don't take this the wrong way."

Mike squinted in confusion. "Then, why the hassle?" He asked. The room suddenly got an air of dread, the hairs on the back of his neck raised in response.

Charles made a motion with his hands to his goons as he continued. "It's who she was after that caught our attention. This girl, Hachi-?" He scanned Mike's careful nod, "-her tastes in targets are high indeed. We would like to meet with her."

Mike's thoughts were scrambling for a way out of this 'interrogation.' Much so that he barely heard the reptile's next question. "Who is she?"

"I don't know her beyond her name and that she came from overseas," He answered honestly. "Charles, I can't get her to come to you. She doesn't listen to threats, and I bet she has the skills to fight anyone you send. Sorry."

With a simple wave from his captor's hand, the equine bodyguard came in for a persuasion. "I must have something in my ear because I thought I thought I heard that you couldn't help us," Charles said cheerfully, smiling broadly as his bodyguard backhanded Michael across the nose.

Pain shot through to his brain and Michael gritted his teeth, wiping the blood onto his wrist. He remained silent. The reptile sighed and nodded his head. A large fist struck Mike in the collarbone. He could feel his bones pop from the compressive force. He actually thought he heard a sound, like the sound of a breaking bone. The ferret yelped in pain; then the other hand clamped his mouth shut. With his noise subdued, the assailant resumed his assault, landing targeted blows at spots known to inflict acute pain. Mike's legs twitched with every blow, aching excruciatingly.

"I could watch this all day," Charles' mused in a delightful tone. Eventually, Mike relented. At that point, he was covered in bruises and spitting blood. They gave him fresh clothes, dressed his wounds and sent him off with a taxi. His head spun, and there was a ringing in his ears. The street lights blazed like suns. He wondered if they caused permanent damage. For a while at first, when they had dropped him off, he kept seeing two where there was one. He had to wait a while for his sight to clear a bit. A beaten he had taken; that too, for a cause that doesn't stand to benefit him. Yet, he felt like he was doing something right.

Hachi was waiting by the restaurant door to meet Mike for dinner. She preferred the sidewalk despite the weather and stood outside by the smoking section, absently listening to a few people trying to flirt with her. Those were flies at a free dinner table, something to be put up with. She spotted the cab pulls in and watched Mike half spill out into the street. His pace staggered, even as he made an effort to disguise that. But his face was a tell that gave his front away.

"Are you okay?" She asked.

Her date gave a reassuring wave. "Fine, really. Just sprained my ankle at work. One of the new hires lost control of his cart and slammed me accidentally." He nearly stumbled towards the door. Again, he staved off her help, entering before her and calling for a server.

Hachi could tell when someone was lying, an instinct from her training. But it needed no genius to see through the lies Mike was living at that moment. She was sure it had something to do with her, but she also sensed that he wouldn't say. She watched him go in, putting enormous effort to stabilize his pace. She went in after in, knowing there was nothing she could to change the way of things.

The two sat on a small table in the rustic-style restaurant smelling of spiced meats and Mediterranean specialties. The kitchen close behind was open to them. Hachi observed several chefs busy filling orders. As soon as their drinks arrived, Mike downed his liquor quickly and pressed the glass to his temple.

She could tell that he was hiding something. "Tell me," she said simply. The battered businessman glanced at her then immediately shut his eyes. He winced from the shining overhead fixtures. That was it; he was not going to share. "Fine then. What are you getting?"

"What?" She saw him tapping on a laminated menu card. "Oh, uh, I don't know."

He was forced to open his eyes to skim his own sheet. She pulled it away from his face. His cheek was swollen, and his lip was split. As he tried to talk, Hachi saw that his mouth had gotten injured. It looked bad, and Hachi could see that they cause him pain. It would have taken quite an assault to cause all that, and Hachi swallowed at remembering how painful that would be. She was a trained pain inflictor herself, and she knew Mike had been struck in places that would break anybody untrained. Mike caught her assessing his condition. "Bad business, partner," he dismissed.

"I thought your company was very hands off."

"It is." Mike straightened himself up. "Do you want to keep talking about this or can we please move on to dinner?" She put up her hands, dropping the subject out of courtesy. Soon, the

23

food came, which was pleasant to her tastes. They ate their entrées in silence. The silence was not all too appealing. Growing uncomfortable under this forced mood, Mike resumed speaking more relevant business.

"Your snooping a few days ago gave us a clue about Lockhardt. I looked into your info to see what you were getting into and believe me; this is an exclusive party. You will need an invitation, meaning Lockhardt or one of his trusted associates has to know you personally. Of course, that is out of the question. I've read that there's electronic, military-grade security which would neutralize you outside of the compound. Beyond that, it's still a mystery to me." He dabbed a napkin to his mouth. "I apologize for not knowing much else."

"You should be more careful." Hachi gave him a firm look. "I appreciate you helping me, but you really don't have to go this far."

Mike cleared his throat; he subtly winked to show his gratitude to the shinobi for caring about his safety. She had no idea how far down that lane he already was.

"It's alright. Anyway, my suggestion for getting to the party is to come across an invitation. I'll talk to some people, find someone who won't ask too many questions. I'll give you a call once I do." He shakily rose to pay the tab, an obvious sign that the meal was over, at least for him.

They put on their jackets and walked out to a line of parked taxis and anticipating customers. Hachi gave one last glance at Mike before she stepped in the vehicle. He wore a grin that she knew was meant to ease her mind. Hachi saw that this was starting to get dangerous for her new friend. She imagined if things went south, someone would see the evidence, draw connections and if they weren't an idiot, crack down on anybody foreign. Mike was suicidal to get involved, but wise to continue with several sides threatening his life.

He closed the door, turned to the night with hands in his pockets. He had his head up, undaunted by whatever had happened to him. He was way past pity, Hachi had none. Still, it felt odd to see him suffer for something she had unwillingly dragged him into. Hachi watched him disappear behind her, feeling some regret for being responsible for his predicament. She wished Torenu was here. He'd know what to do about this.

***

The day before the big celebration, the ferret girl got a call from Michael. He transferred the line over to Dency soon after affirming that it was a secure line. Mike passed out in his office chair as soon as he was off the line. The uppity lizard outlined the building layout, going into scant detail for 'reasons of invested interest.' Hachi listened, committing the plans to memory while jotting down notes on a spiral at the flat. Her pen marks were bold, biting deep into the paper as Dency continued to elaborate. The informant's attitude bled through the receiver, testing the limits of Hachi's patience, made worse by her tendency to go off on tangents about her personal life.

However, she quickly bit back the sarcasm boiling up inside of her and accepted the disguise her new friend was offering. Radley Burns of Burns Insurance was a womanizer. His arm was always occupied by his most recent fancy, and he had many through his career. But, as Ms. Dency put it: "Burns had an quarrel with his date for the party, not more than an hour ago. With a good word and some... well, let's call it sweet talk, I got you booked in as a replacement." Hachi balled her fist on the table. She tolerated a little more chatter to dig the time for her pick up and then slammed the phone down.

"What a bitch!" She spat out loud. She briefly considered adding the lizard to her list of targets after this was all done, leering at the thought.

She looked at the information on the paper. Her fonts were awkward and delved too deep into the paper. Any more force and the pen would have pierced through. She had held the pen tightly like her life depended on it. Somehow, Hachi doubted if the argument between Burns and his dinner date had been natural. She had a sense that Dency was the type to get things done, irrespective of who was hurt or expended. Hachi knew it was none of her business since it means she could now gain entrance to the event. If she doesn't start making preparation right off, she might end up wasting this opportunity.

It was a black car that pulled up outside of her apartment soon after to fetch her for the party. A chauffeur stepped out and opened a door for her with a muted "Good evening." Hachi braced herself for the person she was going to be stuck with for the next hour. Even before the door was closed behind her, the ferret prepared for the arm that she couldn't refuse. Burns, an older chipmunk wiped the champagne off his whiskers. His orange color was beginning to fade, particularly around the muzzle and the inside of his neck where he covered it with a tie. He had glasses on, ones she could tell were for nearsightedness judging from the way his gaze drifted to her outline. Once beside him, he quickly slipped a palm to her waist and beamed gleefully.

"I see your agent does not exaggerate." His clever remark fell on deaf ears as he laughed to himself. Hachi fought to avoid losing her composure. The ride itself felt too long in her opinion. Buildings turned from skyscrapers to high-end estate homes. She half-answered the rodent's casual questions while she stared outside the window at her surroundings. Exotic cars in sleek shapes displayed behind wrought iron fences, next to sweeping roofs and graceful gardens more lavish than any she had seen since her childhood years in Nihon. The wealth of this community was staggering to her. 'Capitalist royalty' was the only term she could think of to describe it. At the very least, this event was being held elsewhere than the cramped metropolis.

Shortly after arriving, Hachi was confident that she could navigate a mansion better than an office. As it was, a monolith of steel and stone designed in modern taste stood like the castle Hachi had worked in before. Its sleek outer walls seamlessly joined to a thin glass pane, the roof merely starting where the blocky contour stopped rising, hedges cultivated between ornate flower beds and a fountain illuminated by pool lights. The design made it certain to make sneaking by quite difficult. While she had yet to see it, Hachi expected to encounter a surveillance system. Stiff as a board, she let her 'date' saddle them past security so she could to see just how a tycoon such as Lockhardt lived.

Inside the coatroom, she had to improvise a facade to stash her gear that she would come back for after some reconnaissance. A catering parade of chefs and entertainers spilled out into a high dome-shaped banquet hall within the exterior architecture. An oversized chandelier from up high gave a cool white light, which complimented the wall scones evenly spaced along the halls. Aesthetic was everywhere. A long table took the far end of the room, laden with hors-d'oeuvres. Modest speakers played contemporary music while crisp busboys carried trays between the various attendees. Across the room, rich socialites in lavishing tuxedos with their partners filled the room, chatting and laughing graciously as aristocrats do. Radley steered them towards a distinct group. Someone there recognized him; a stout, calm pug cradling a dainty wine glass.

"Ah, Burns. Never alone. How was the drive? Did you blow off the card I sent you?"

"It smelled too cheap," Burns responded, letting his hand drop just a little. "Besides, I had more important things to do anyway." The portly canine pulled his gaze away from Hachi's fuchsia dress with some effort. He stood some centimeters shorter than Radley, who was then only a smidgen taller than her. "What's this all about?" The rodent asked while pointing at a nearby talkative group of felines behind him.

The pug didn't turn around. "Hedge funds. They're economists trying to get as many investors as they can to buy into a volatile stock."

"High risk, high reward," said one of the cats who joined in. Beneath Hachi's young, attractive features she was growing unbearably bored.

"Please, Thomas," Radley laughed. "Let's discuss this later if not sometime next week. I think my companion is starting to nod off."

"Very well then, would you kindly depart from us, good sir?" Thomas shooed the stockbroker off, returning to a light conversation with Radley without giving him another thought.

Most of it was tasteless jokes, which Hachi was forced to humor much to her chagrin. Throughout that time, she made a note of the staff routines, including the different paths going in and out of the hall. Dency might not have given her any blueprints, but she was determined to scope out her target without attracting any unwanted suspicion. First, she had to get free from the sleazebag attached to her. She acted her part, handing him glass after glass until he leaned his weight onto her. Nobody suspected her to be anything more than a bored escort.

When she felt he was drunk enough, she spoke a few choice words to his ear, and Radley stumbled off to the bathroom, doggedly anticipating. He never saw Hachi's fist coming, it sent a reeling blow to his temple, putting him out for the evening. Now alone in the empty room, the ferret dragged Mr. Burns' unconscious, snoring body into the toilet and propped his head against the porcelain bowl. Afterward, she went straight to work.

Exiting the restroom, she nonchalantly made her way back to the closet for the coatroom to retrieve her bag. Nobody gave her a second glance as she slipped into the coatroom and came out with a large purse – it was amazing what these "civilized" people would overlook. Simply by carrying herself inconspicuously, she evaded suspicion from their eyes. Heading into an empty study, the shinobi stripped off the dress and put on her smuggled suit and weapons.

Hachi had not seen Lockhardt once during the entire time downstairs. This nearly raised some small red flags for her but it didn't matter now though. Her plan was already in action, and there was no pulling out. She would just have to tackle the mission on her feet.

Hachi decided to take advantage of the higher ceilings on the second floor. Watching for cameras, she made her way into the less occupied sections of the villa. Below her, a hallway of white laminate had a guard pacing. He carried nothing out in the open, clad in suit and tie per custom should he be called from his shift. The ninja gauged his movements, sweating a bit. Pulling out a kunai, she positioned herself for a deadly takedown. Suddenly, a loud crash came from a different part of the building, which threw her off balance and alerted the guard to run towards her position. Her cover was blown, and Hachi knew to act fast.

"Hey!" shouted the guard, about to draw his firearm. Acting fast, Hachi threw her kunai at him slicing open his neck, covering the white hallway in a spray of blood. He fell to the floor with a thud. Hachi had nothing to do to the noise his fallen body made.

What the hells was that noise? Hachi wondered. This job just became more difficult and complicated. The ferret girl had no time to worry if her cover was blown or to change plans. She dashed down the hall, devoid of any further security, passing by sets of doors with nameplates above them. Then, at the end of the hallway, which her instincts told her was overlooking the front garden, a final set of double doors caught her eye. A brass plate, aged artificially, had the text 'Private Conference' engraved on it. That had to be it, the ferret girl convinced herself. She decided to check it out, Lockhart must be hiding behind those doors.

The shinobi closed the gap, drawing her blade for an ambush. She threw a few glances around, careful not to let down her guard. No one came, so she approached carefully. No noise, not even from the event right below her. With the coast clear, she squared herself in front of the door to crack it open even as something inside of her began to feel odd about it.

Without warning, a gloved hand gripped her wrist from within. Hachi swung at it with her wakizashi, but it was repelled by strange feedback as if she had tried to cut through metallic armor. She cursed her luck for a moment, blaming whatever made her proceeded against her sudden instinctive oddness. Trapped, another hand on her blind spot from around the door grasped her higher up. Struggling blindly, she was pulled inside.

CHAPTER 3

Two Foxes

Spartan chairs and a technicolor rug spun past Hachi as she careened into a potted tree. She had just been flung across the room like a sack of meat. Her sight blurred for a moment as a figure rushed towards her from behind the door. Hachi saw a glint of the steel wire it carried, reflecting off of the overhead lights.

The opponent swept at her legs, but she rolled forward, negating the strength of the blow and the threat of her opponent's razor wire. Catching one of her assailant's legs, she twisted it until she heard the cracking sound of a dislocated knee. Her foe – a male, judging by his physique and voice, grunted in pain. The fight had not gone out of him, however, and he forced his weight on her, trying to turn the tables. He threw a jab at her upper back before propping himself with his other hand, trying to align the metallic strand around her head. Pain welled up where his blow landed, but her taut muscle dampened the effect to a degree. Still, there was the wire to avoid.

Fighting to get off the floor, Hachi capitalized on his wounded knee. She sent a back kick at the knee, putting a lot of force into it. The action wrenched the knee further. In response, he roared in agony and dropped the wire, clawing at her eyes in a vain attempt to shake her off but she turned her head away before he could reach them.

In a fit of desperation, the attacker again lashed out with his fist, striking her at the ear, sending her reeling in pain, eardrum ringing. He pulled her back down but she held on tightly, and they both went tumbling on the floor. Both wrestled in a flurry of punches, kicks and jockeying for free weapons. The shinobi's sword was still by the plant, and her knife was buried in the previous guard, long out of reach. She had to find a weapon quick, anything within reach.

She maneuvered against the holds he attempted to subdue her with, reaching around her for anything sharp or heavy to use against him. Her hand latched onto his belt, and she ripped away an object the size of an apple. Her foe showed no notice of this and Hachi had no time to figure out what she had grabbed. Taking the initiative, the ferret girl slammed the orb against his neck. His hold on her slackened, and she finally wriggled herself free. Her opponent pushed himself back onto his feet, crimson eyes gleaming with the intent to kill. The ninja swore she saw death dancing wildly from his gaze.

Hachi quickly scanned her surroundings. The room itself was smaller than she had expected, ten feet squared and furnished by a hardwood desk that didn't quite fit Lockhardt's usual decorative aesthetics. Her target was nowhere to be seen; just this red fox who had been lying in wait. The fight was not over. With a wild look, he pulled out some sort of club and was limping towards her. She took a breath to relax her muscles and calm her mind down some.

Her thoughts were racing. Where in blazes was Lockhardt? Had she been set up by that shifty lizard? Or was Lockhardt just the kind of paranoiac who hires trained killers to lie in wait behind every door? She wouldn't put it beyond Dency to betray her, as unlikely as it seems. The questions in her mind vanished as the club that her foe held crackled like lightning. The flickering bluish aura it radiated revealed more of his visage. This time,

Hachi has no plans to get tagged by anymore of his attacks. His jaw was parted slightly, showing his small, grit teeth set in a deadly lock. His eyes hid behind a pair of blackened spectacles that complimented his formal wear. Two dark ears folded back in an involuntary response to danger. Hachi had never seen these foreigners using lightning magic before, but she knew enough about it to avoid letting the weapon touch her at all costs.

He kept careful note of the distance between the ferret and her weapon, still stuck behind the plant, trying to nick her with his baton. Now and then, he lurched forward with the object, trying to jolt the ferret, who merely sidestepped away to escape his blows. Hachi was slowly but steadily forced to give up ground in order to continue dodging. She was being forced back into a corner. He was confident, clinical, never overreaching. Intuitively reacting to her counters, unlike any fighter she had faced before.

At last, her back was pressed to the wall. It was time to act. Now or never.

Having her cornered, he never would have expected what would happen next. Running on pure instinct, she pushed back behind her and closed the distance between them both as he struck again, albeit a moment too late. The club tapped her off her shoulder, singeing a small spot of her outfit and the fur underneath. Immense pain followed the sizzling sound as the material curled and burned. However, she had secured a firm grasp on his weapon's hilt. Utilizing her momentum, she twisted it out of his grip before tossing it out of the office window. Then, running on adrenalin, Hachi made a beeline to retake her weapon and bring the fight outside. He saw what she was doing and gave chase, but was slowed by his injured leg and he failed to catch her in time. Once she snapped her weapon back up, she bolted for the door, her pursuer close behind.

Meanwhile, Radley, still drunk sullen and toped as he was, had found himself being forced out by two muscle-headed security personnel. His clothes were drenched in sweat, his legs felt weak, and the sides of his face were hot as if he had experienced an allergic reaction. They were outside near the entrance, trudging towards his awaiting vehicle with other guests departing in similar fashions. He tried to question what the ruckus was about, but his words were slurred to the point of being incomprehensible. After they dropped him into the rear seat and closed the car door, he briefly wondered what became of his date. Had she left him? He couldn't remember, but it wasn't like it mattered much to the mogul. There were plenty of pretty young things out there to take her place. *Good riddance.*

In a quieter wing of the compound, Benjamin Lockhardt was holed up inside of his private study. His mind was tense when he learned that there was an intruder who was after him. Unaccustomed to threats against his person, he was hyperventilating, clutching a pistol in his quivering hands as he waited for the all-clear. The signal was taking too long and this did nothing to help calm his nerves. He held the gun more tightly, feeling a bead of sweat trickling down his forehead. Despite that, the hyena counted himself lucky. There, in the cover of a prestigious gathering, he had prepared this last minute security measure with a certain contractor who reached out to him some time prior.

The private contracting company in question operated in complete obscurity, through offshore banking accounts and shell companies. Employing a cadre of lawyers and accountants alongside their more conventional forces, the PMC could promise no government would ever find anything amiss with the transactions between themselves and their clientele. This impressed Lockhardt enough to trust their agent, a man who called himself "Miles." Whoever he really was didn't matter much to the businessman, Miles was paid well enough to do his job and keep his mouth shut. Lockhardt didn't pry either, his associates have testified how skilled his choice of a last resort line of defense was after a few small time jobs. Later on, they had met face-to-face to discuss job-related matters, and he found his hire to be an enjoyable conversationalist as well as a reliable retainer.

Suddenly, his ruminations were cut short when he heard a noise coming from the proximity speaker. His monitors outside had detected something where there should have been no activity. His strategic location was meant to place him out of harm's reach easily and kept him close to multiple escape routes as well. Lockhardt paused for the safe word but all his ears picked up was silence. He pushed a section of the wall, then slid a panel to access a security feed that was wired to the camera located outside of the room's exit. A wire rack made of steel stood among boxes of paper nearby where his secret entrance was. In effect, it was invisible to anyone passing by since it was cleverly hidden behind a false layer of sheetrock. He pressed a series of commands, and the screens came alive. However, he picked no one up in the visuals. Rather, he heard a cracking sound like the opening of a door. He turned to look at the door. It was still closed. Odd to say the least.

Not knowing where that noise came from, he waited tensely until the door unexpectedly clicked open. Someone was entering, and Lockhardt's muscles froze as a chill ran down his spine. A gloved hand carrying a small gun was the first thing he saw followed by a feminine figure, unlike the one he saw Miles fighting near the garden. She panned the room that he was watching. The hyena held his breath, hoping that she would leave. His heart was racing, and despite his held breath, he felt the sound of his racing heart would draw her near. He felt uneasy, the hyena's stomach tied in knots as sweat dripped from his brow. He noticed that his neck was still taught, his upper body was still flexing while his legs weren't in the best position to bolt anywhere. He tried to curl his bicep. It didn't move. He was stunned, for all practical purposes. He almost screamed when his elbow cramped up, the tendons contracting painfully from fear. Lockhardt tried to take slow breaths, but again his body was disobeying him. His heart and lungs felt like they were going to explode. Staying silent in the near darkness of his safe room, Lockhardt watched his monitor as the fox woman strolled ever closer to his hiding spot, and laid a hand over the loose plate.

Riddled by pain, Lockhardt huddled against the wall, holding his head in his hands. He did not know what the female outside was up to, nor did he care. All he wanted was for this skank to leave. What exactly was he paying his security for, if not to prevent exactly this situation? He started to claw at his face, maddened by fear and impotent anger. Driven by his base fury, he drew blood from himself. Crimson fluid flowed down, soiling his suit with sticky scarlet. The pain seemed to recede shortly, the hyena himself felt numb and increasingly fainter. The last thought that crossed his mind before the torture resumed and realizing that she was behind this supernatural assault from the start.

The white fox that penetrated Lockhardt's safe room had an odd air about her. Her purple eyes seem to glow as she reached out with her mind, scanning for the hyena. She felt a tug on her mental tether, drawing her eyes towards a particular section of the wall. Her net had been cast methodically, closing in on the businessman since the start of the party, and now she had him trapped and helpless. She could sense the venom that coursed within him, could feel his mind tear itself apart in a panicked frenzy. She approached the hidden door slowly, waiting for his writhing and clawing to subside. Finally, sensing that the arms dealer had stopped thrashing and was now unconscious, she ceased her mental assault.

Hachi focused on putting more distance between herself and her attacker. Still running, she slapped her arm awake where his electrical baton had made contact. The pain coursed through her shoulder, removing the numb feeling. After she felt better, her top priority right now was to get out in one piece. This would be the first mission in her career that was a failure, but she would at least escape alive. She needed to regroup and come up with a new plan. That fox who she encountered was too good to be taken on by herself. She needed a comrade, like Junior.

Unable to match Hachi's speed, the agent drew a blocky plastic gun and fired something at her from behind. Steel prongs raced through the air, with trailing thin wires. She nearly got one in her back but turned at a corner at the last second. She never looked back, placing all her attention to finding a way out. By her reckoning, the doors on the right of the hallway all lead to rooms adjacent to the outside. Praying that Lockhardt hadn't posted assassins in every room in this house, she picked a door at random and wrenched it open.

To her relief, nobody awaited the ferret on the other side of the door, but she was faced with another problem. The room she had entered was a windowless office, barely decorated beyond a few bookshelves and a desk with one of those plastic boxes that people used for work – she faintly recalls it being called a *konpyuta*. That wasn't important. In moments, she would be cornered again, but at least she has her blade ready. She strained her ears, waiting for footsteps that never sounded. Her blade on guard, she waited a few minutes before it became clear that no one was coming.

Hachi realized that she was wasting valuable time. By now, that bodyguard had probably called in backup. She had to leave. By the time the ninja's adrenaline had worn off, the bruises on her started their flaring pain. Her body felt hot. She swore under her breath, peering through the crack under the door, but seeing nothing. She threw it open, diving out and towards the direction she had come, hoping to catch him before he could put a bullet in her, but there was nobody there. Coming back to the corner of the hallway, Hachi peered around to see her pursuer trying to break down another door, with little success. Not noticing her, he cursed, placing a small tan object on the door's latch. He took several steps down the hallway. Seemingly satisfied that some arbitrary distance had been crossed, he made a motion like checking for a pulse on his wrist, and all of a sudden, an explosion erupted from the door. The agent did not wait for the smoke to fully clear. His gun at the ready, he breached the room. Hachi thought to tail him, not wanting him to get out of her sight, but he doubled back to the entrance before she had a chance to move, firing gunshots inside the room, then in the hallway as he backed up with practiced steps, never losing his aim. He released the magazine from his gun, replacing it with honed ease.

By the doorway, another stranger charged him, trying to catch him in a grapple. The male dropped his empty weapon, raising his fists like a trained boxer. The ferret, eager to exploit this situation, charged his blind side with her blade drawn. He shifted, picked up the white-clad snow fox by the abdomen and flung her in front of the shinobi. Hachi took a blind swing, not really caring who got hit. The edge cut into the floor with a hard clang as the two foxes separated to avoid it. Blood dripped on the ground as the two clashed again, trading kicks and punches with increasing ferocity. The red fox threw a left at the white fox. She parried the blow, launching a counter with a straight jab at the red fox's abdomen. He was well prepared as he fended off the blow. The miss threw the white fox off balance, and she quickly twists to regain her stance. It was a move too late, the red fox found an opening and landed a devastating punch on the white fox's solar plexus, and she crumpled to the ground.

Hachi danced around, slicing her weapon erratically at him while he warded her off with his hands. The suit he wore had been shredded several times, revealing plated armor over his whole body. He caught the shinobi's thrust with his elbow, pulling her off balance and knocking the sword away from her hands. The other female was still down, and Hachi assumed she was possibly dead. But the red fox ducked for his gun, back into that room, pushing someone else. The figure was familiar, and a recognition glinted in Hachi's eyes…

41

"Lockhardt!" Hachi yelled as she went for her target. She lurched with skill and purpose, determined not to let him escape, undaunted by the bullet darting out of the red fox's gun. Pulling the slide back, the bodyguard shot at her again. Hachi jumped back and forth, the bullets whizzing by. She went for Lockhardt once more, but the red fox had reloaded, covering Lockhardt so he could flee out of her sight. His aim grew less accurate, and the ferret could see now that his arm was bleeding from under his clothes. The agent's expression though was one of calculated, unmoving concentration. He backed up five paces, firing the remainder of his clip as he does. Then with his ammunition spent, he spun on his heels and retreated. He had gotten his prize to safety, and now without a means of defense.

Hachi had a mind to press on the attack. Her will demanded her mission to be completed at any cost, but she was in no shape to go on. She stood panting in anger at her injuries, watching the red fox disappear behind the side of the villa, Lockhardt's leather shoes slapping against the pavement as he ran wildly for his life, his now loosened shirt flailing behind him as he fled. She had to leave before more trouble arrived. Hachi knew that was what Torenu would say at this outcome. Lockhardt had likely tripped an alarm, and it wouldn't be long until this place would be crawling with goons. She had to vacate now, get back to Michael and figure out the next step. Hachi glanced at the strange fox woman for a moment before running to retrieve her sword where it had landed.

Once her digits had grabbed hold of the sword, the female vulpine had lunged for her. Hachi turned with her back facing the floor having the sword outwards. She had hoped that the white fox would run into it, but with a hiss, she backed off, making it so Hachi could jump back onto her feet. The two stood there gasping for breath. Hachi herself feeling her lungs giving way as she tried to look around, but the white fox didn't seem to be making a move at all. Too tired to do anything and the clock ticking before this place will be teeming with the enemy, she swore under her breath.

Hachi could hear the incoming reinforcements' footsteps. Without a second thought, she started to run off to the side down the hallway. Looking behind her, she could see Lyssa having trouble getting away. She was still reeling from the effect of her bashing from the red fox. The ferret was now fighting against her better nature. While it had been her fault that this mishap had happened in the first place, something about leaving the white fox seemed wrong. There were also these tall walls to get over. Hachi was under the sudden realization that she would not be able to get out on her own.

Turning back to Lyssa, she grabbed the taller lady by the hand and tugged her into another alley. "If you help me get out, I'll help you," Hachi said as the breathless white fox nodded in reply. She shut her mouth and stood up straight, the ferret and her were now under a sort of understanding. Hachi just hoped she hadn't messed up so much that tracking Benny again would be impossible. Sneering at the thought, the two prepared themselves to find an escape. They were not sure which way was best exit strategy or what type of reinforcements were being deployed. Still, they had to get moving.

They dash off in the opposite direction of the approaching footsteps, Hachi holding on to the white fox to give her support. She appeared to be self-rejuvenating or perhaps had a means to suppress her own pain. They came to the end of a hall where a door leans slightly opened. Hachi peered out, to be sure that the area was clear of anybody. Seeing none, the ninja girl signaled at Lyssa to proceed. While safety was not guaranteed, there was no better choice than to go ahead.

Both of them made a break for it, the white fox noticeably going faster than Hachi, much to the Takaro's surprise. Taking up the front, they both heard gunfire from behind. Bullet whizzed passed them with a rush. The ferret puffed laboriously while keeping up with the white fox's movements. Jumping between buildings and vanishing at one point before the ferret could catch up to her, she noticed that some force was letting her perform such feats. Her physique certainly did not hint at rigorous training like Hachi's was. This stranger was athletic, but not much else. Something was propelling her, like an internal force or something of the sort.

They rounded a corner, seeing the exit's opening further down. The fox kept her lead with the ferret on her heels. They were halfway down the final stretch when a group of reinforcements rounded the corner up front. Quick as a wink, the white fox tosses the ferret over the building away from their range and followed suit. Fresh shots of the bullet ricocheted off the surfaces around them. At this point, the two were running on fumes, but safety was their top priority. Shoes pounded against the pavement underneath them as finally, Lyssa grabbed hold of Hachi's hand to hoist her onto higher ground.

"Thanks..." The white fox responded rather quietly, in between catching her breath. Not talking much else after that. Hachi discovered, however, the reason she had spoken—because they finally made their way out. Out on the other side, Hachi lead Lyssa through the hills below. This was far better than being captured, or worse, killed.

CHAPTER 4

Alliance

A few hours had passed since the failed raid on Lockhardt's mansion. Now with her new 'friend,' Hachi considered the present situation. The snow fox known as Lyssa stared off blankly, lost in her own thoughts. The esper had the social graces of an ice block. Hachi hadn't received so much as a proper thanks for helping her get out. Lockhardt's soirée was filled with unsavory characters – greedy and corrupt, all jostling for a little more money or power. They, however, at least had the decency to try and hide it, even if they did a poor job. Lyssa, on the other hand, wore her irritation on her sleeve. The two had nearly come to blows after escaping together.

To make matters worse, Mike barely managed to evacuate the two of them in time. It took a few phone calls before he picked up, and the ferret girl fumbled and cursed at the unfamiliar device with each missed call. When he eventually answered, his voice was muffled and strained, but he jot down the details and promised to show up soon. Finally, he arrived, looking almost as ragged and disheveled at the two women. Too tired to ask any questions about Hachi's new accomplice, he ushered them in and took off, wanting to put as much space between the mansion guards and the three of them. As they drove in silence, Mike yawned to stay awake; Lyssa shut her eyes in meditation and Hachi did her best to stay calm and optimistic.

The foreign landscape passed by in a blur, and Hachi found

herself too dazed to appreciate the view. Her mind drifted as she rested her head against the window. The fancy abodes of the elite gave way to cheap, run-down suburbs as they drew closer to the city. The landscape, rushing by against the vehicle, presented her with no fascination either, although she found the transition somewhat intriguing. From high-end estate with alluring courtyards hidden away in the silence of the countryside to slowly easing back into chaotic, rusty and rowdy jam-packed suburban houses. Such disparity, the cool and chilling air of the elite outskirts slowly but increasingly gaining heat as their descent to the urbs deepens.

The difference in values between Nihon and Pennotia further troubled her. Around here, it seemed that the exploitation of common folk was normal. Hachi thought of her own home, her family's household. Sure, they had servants...but they were more than that too. Her family fought against the system bringing war on everyone. Right? Her mind curled into itself, eating at the doubt caused by a shift in perspective that Hachi was struggling hard to make sense of. The bureaucracy, and the uncaring corporations pushing a working class to its limit like a whip cracking on a broken, bloody back, made her sick. She had seen what Mike suffered through, simply for stepping out of line, and how he just accepted it like it was his due. The masses here endured abuse and near slavery because they knew nothing better. Regretfully, as much as her mind railed against the injustices in this new land, she had to put those thoughts aside. She must find Lockhardt as soon as possible to get to this "Dark One" in order to end this all.

They pulled off the road into an alley parking stall, knocking over some trash bins, which spilled their smelly innards onto the pavement. Mike put the car in park and turned his head to the rearview mirror, brushing his face thoughtfully. Lyssa's eyes darted between her two new acquaintances, but she kept silent.

"Come on," he said. They all piled out. Mike checked the time, Hachi stretched her arms, and Lyssa stood by quietly, eerily blending with the dreary background. The male ferret cleared his throat and flicked his chin towards their destination. It was a dingy looking storefront with dusty windows casting dulled yellow light while the tiled, slant covers above gave the impression of heavy eyelids. There was a slight draft flowing between the buildings, causing a number of paper bags to fly down towards the way of the group. A plaque made of sheet steel with the word "Earl's" stamped on it hung above the main entrance. Hachi looked around and saw a few other cars in the cramped lot hugging the indent of the mini-mart on the adjacent side. Mike pushed ahead, and they followed him past the creaking wooden frame and inside the bar, where a familiar smell of food and people greeted their noses.

The first thing to hit them was the aroma of a vintage wine. Despite the run-down appearance on the outside, Earl's was actually a well-kept eatery on the inside. The establishment had mostly tables, but a few booths did take up the far end. Mike guided them to one of the booths, wasting no time ushering them to a private place to talk. Hachi had a good view of the establishment from her spot. There was a haze of smoke lingering around their section in particular. Everything appeared a tiny bit out of focus, warming their appearances, softening the wear inflicted on them.

The Takaro, as usual, took the time to scan the setting and the view from their station. From the corner of her eye, she caught the esper doing the same with short, calculated glances. She was just like her, in a way. Mike didn't seem to notice though. The salaryman merely settled down in his chair to go about business. He picked up a pinned leather menu and slipped it across to her.

47

"I take it the operation went wrong." He remarked. Hachi looked up at Mike from the sparsely cropped page.

"Given my lack of information and other complications, I have to admit that I got overwhelmed. Why didn't your contact tell me he had such forces?"

"More than likely it was because she either didn't know or assumed you would have expected such level of security," Mike replied. "Quite unfortunate how it turned out, but at least you're still in one piece. What exactly happened there anyway?"

Hachi gave him a condensed, yet comprehensive account starting from her infiltration, followed by her search around the villa, up to her escape with Lyssa after their fight with the red fox. His ears perked up at how remarkable it sounded. "So," he said, trying to picture the encounter in his head, "Lockhardt had an unforeseen trump card. This bodyguard seems to be well-trained to be able to fend off the two of you." He motioned towards Lyssa at the last part of his sentence whom remained mute on the issue.

"Now I'm not sure if Benjamin has another agent lined up when I go after him again." Hachi cupped her chin analytically. "He escaped, so he must be using this chance to fill the cracks in his security. I will need better intel than what I initially had. No half-baked nonsense and hearsay. If it involves my mission, being prepared is literally a matter of life or death."

An earthy, blusterous hare with his ears pinned back came and took their orders. He whisked off as soon as he had come, after writing down their choices. Michael wound up ordering for their silent guest and Hachi, who was nearly starving after her exertion that night, had ordered a steak. After a while, Mike became concerned about the newest addition to their little party. She still hadn't said a word, and he was beginning to wonder if

48

she was suffering from a stroke. Her fur color, almost albino, made her look exotic. Her features were rigid but feminine. She wore a wrap of white cloth around her head, letting it follow the natural path her hair took, and it cinched tight just above the neck. She looked off vacantly at first, but took notice of Mike's concerned stare and turned her head to glare straight back into his eyes.

"Hello? You there?" he asked her, unsure if she understood him or not.

"She hasn't said much since I met her," Hachi told him. "Not the nicest way to treat someone who rescued you."

"She might not be able to, you know." Mike offered. "Wait a minute." He fumbled in his suit pocket for a few moments, fishing out a pen and a notepad. He held them out to the silent arctic fox, who remained motionless. Frustrated but still determined to get her communicating, he uncapped the pen and set both it and the notepad in front of her. "Please, can you tell us why you were after Lockhardt?"

Lyssa picked up the pen, slowly turning it over in her hands, and Hachi imagined she was contemplating how effective it would be as a weapon. After a long, drawn-out silence, she spoke. Her voice was quiet but firm. "That's classified information."

Hachi seethed in her seat as something sparked in her brain. "Come on!" She growled, her patience at an end. "I saved your hide, so help us out! I need Lockhardt." She was moments away from just decking the aggravating fox in front of the whole restaurant.

"I don't care about your needs," Lyssa stated, very matter-of-factly. Her tone was as emotionless as her expression, suggesting an air of indifference to Hachi's plight. This fruitless exchange was visibly frustrating Hachi. Mike caught her hair rising and the way her fist on the table clenched, itching for release. He reached over the table and placed his hand on hers. The fox girl looked away.

"You better listen--!" She was about to go on a tirade but was stopped in time by Mike. The ninja girl felt him gave her hand a little squeeze. She understands that he meant for her to calm down. In some way, she also felt that violence would not take them far but still, she didn't appreciate how this new girl was acting towards their hospitality.

"This is getting us nowhere. I risked much helping you get away from that mansion by driving you both out of there so it would be nice to know how much trouble I've gotten myself into." Mike said bluntly. "Look, I'll tell you why we were there if you'll reciprocate."

He glanced at Hachi, squeezing her hand again before she could ruin any attempts to resolve this amicably. The ferret girl nevertheless fumed while Mike explained as much as he can about their previous days spent gathering intel rather crudely, being sure to avoid implicating the organization he had help from. Lyssa glared at him, and he felt a tendril of panic work into his mind. "You're not very honest with me, Mike."

"Yes, I'm leaving out a few minor details, but it's all true. Hachi came here from the land of Nihon, trying to hunt down Lockhardt. His brother had been working for this Dark guy, and we believe Lockhardt is too. Now, will you tell us why you're after the same person like us?"

The white fox took this all in for a moment. She was still under no obligation to tell them anything, but she doubted they would just let her walk away now. Clearly, backing down was not an option for them, no matter the circumstances. Kneading a knot in the wood, the esper fiddled around for a second before she made her decision. Her features softened as she relaxed and tense mood dissipated. Even at that, her expression was firm when she spoke. "You cannot tell a soul," she warned them.

Michael scoffed. "Madam, I've been living on the edge for the past few days. You can't possibly make things any worse, believe me."

Lyssa took a deep breath before letting it go slowly. "Your target has information on an important shipment that my group is in the process of procuring. I was to interrogate him and forward the extracted information to my superiors." The fox's face was wrought with disappointment. She was not even trying to hide it at all.

Hachi interjected, full of interest. "Both of us failed then. But that red fox...the one who took Lockhardt away and fended us off. Do you know anything about him?"

"I was told to expect complications," she replied. "I had it all planned accordingly. You just had to keep him occupied until I was done with Benny."

From the change in Hachi's expression, Mike knew Lyssa shouldn't have said that. Or perhaps, she could have put it a little more mildly. But he figured from the few hours he had spent with her, the esper puts herself above Hachi, very highly too.

"What do you mean by that? Was I just a bait in your grand master plan? How did you even know I was there?" The ferret girl began fuming indignantly towards the snow fox. It amazed her how she was meant to tolerate such a callous and surly fox who is clearly disrespecting her in front of her partner.

The fox nodded. "It almost worked, too." Hachi boiled over, grabbing the table to flip it. Fortunately, it was bolted down securely, so a bar fight was averted. Clenching her fists, Hachi slid out of the booth and stormed out of the restaurant. The ferret has had enough. Damn her, she hates to be used.

Mike tried to grab her wrist, to hold her back, but she was already too far away. "Hachi, wait!" He hissed. Before he could think to do anything else, the waiter returned with their food. Noticing that some conflict had occurred, but having no interest in involving himself, he set the table and beat a hasty retreat as quickly as his legs would carry him, but not before wishing them a pleasant meal.

Not wanting to let his food go to waste, and hungry after a long day at work, Mike dug in. Lyssa, on the other hand, seemed to have no appetite, and simply stared blankly at a space on the back of the booth.

Sated, Mike rested his hands on the table, away from his silverware. "You didn't need to say that, ma'am. You're still here for a reason, right? Otherwise, you could just stand up and walk away."

Lyssa again wore an uneasy frown following his statement. "I failed." The statement oozed negativity and so did her demeanor as her shoulders slumped. She gazed ahead vacuously, lost in deep-seated regret.

Mike was really starting to get annoyed with her negative attitude. "Yes, we know. So what? Do you have a suicide pact for this kind of setback?"

 "What? Of course not," she shot back up at him, miffed.

"Then what in blazes is wrong with you?" Mike demanded, nearly shouting. "I see no reason why you want to stick around with us. None at all. I must be missing something here, or you're the dumbest mercenary I've ever tried to work with." He grabbed his fork and sunk it well into the oily pasta. After a few mouthfuls, he barked at her, "Get with the program or get out. It's all the same to me. I'm through playing games with you."

Lyssa decided to comply and began with an introduction. Her words came fumbling in at first but grew more coherent as kept going. The salaryman got more than he bargained for though, much to his dismay, as she had to start from the very beginning.

More than twenty years ago, EMR readings from the sky sparked a great debate within the country's top government departments. Astrological engineers briefed the president, with undeniable facts, that a celestial body of notable size had entered the atmosphere and would shortly crash land somewhere remote within the Pennotian borders. The president was swift to respond, giving the order for a search party to be assembled immediately. The object ended up in a valley an hour away from the nearest city, spinning a buzz among the locals at first. A considerable amount of money was thrown at the local media to spin a narrative to keep the townspeople from asking too many unwanted questions. It worked, and as soon as the public's excitement faded, the administration's science team settled down and got straight to work.

The scientist team that they deployed found a luminescent glow coming off the vicinity of the crater's epicenter. Precautions were taken to check for radioactivity and toxicity; none was found, and further investigations to move forward ahead of schedule were commenced. Another team was sent to ground zero where they excavated a purplish meteorite and several glowing fragments. One helicopter ride later, it was put under thorough study inside the outpost's research facility.

The meteorite's contents had an idiosyncrasy to them. At approximately one cubic yard in size, it weighed unusually light for its stature. The crystal was dubbed *Nooscite* by its handlers. Most of the research data that had been collected during the first few months by the initial teams had been lost other than the fact that it was not toxic to biological life. Lyssa entered late into the project as a volunteer. The snow fox signed up to quench her desire to work close to something out of this world. She was one of eleven that were chosen for this privilege, undergoing a week of training beforehand. Lyssa felt proud to be of service to her country's future, but looking back, it really was naive of her given how she had turned out.

Donning special-made suits, they were all subject to constant exposure from the extraterrestrial rock in various ways. To them, it was borderline illegal. They inhaled vapors, drank mixtures and even consumed bits of it as instructed. This didn't seem to produce any results so a few days later, some of her colleagues had it injected into their bodies. Several moments later, they collapsed from a seizure that knocked them out for hours. Their eyes had taken on a purple glow, similar to the glow of the Nooscite. Staff in hazmat suits came to check up on them regularly, tending to their dietary needs and hygiene. A week later, two of them were expelled due to being "incompatible," but the rest of them were ready for the next step as their bodies had adapted to the Nooscite. The scientist had a feeling they were getting closer to a ground-breaking discovery that may change the fate of state security.

At this time, Lyssa and the others began to experience symptoms of brief dizziness and addled thoughts as if something was affecting their minds. Still, they kept quiet about this in order to avoid expulsion. Soon after, she began noticing strange occurrences. It felt like a zen moment, based on intuition rather than a focus of the mind. At first, these were mild. Objects moved on their own around her, sometimes flying across the room if she was angry, sometimes sliding towards her if she needed them. She could tell when her colleagues and the scientists were lying or hiding something. Eventually, these abilities were discovered, and they were exactly the kind of breakthrough that her country was hoping for. The buzz surrounding the ones with these abilities changed. The next step focused less about developing their prowess but rather a shift towards learning control.

The fox spent the next half of the year practicing and honing her abilities with the other subjects who had remained. Soon, she was able to read the thoughts of those around her, and even manipulate them to an extent. She could launch an object towards a target as easily as if she was throwing it. At some point, she moved up from training to go on missions for her nation. Sensing the white fox was about to go off on a tangent, Mike interrupted her and brought her focus back to Lockhardt.

Regarding the night's event earlier, Lyssa had been invited under a prepared alias. She was supposed to blend into the crowd like Hachi and search for Lockhardt. If he didn't show then, Lyssa was to proceed up to the restricted private floor and flush him out. "I would have preferred it be over with quickly, but the target made it harder than expected by employing Deltus."

"Hey, it could be worse. Hachi helped you get out fine, right?"

"Absolutely not. I had failed my mission, and the agent overpowered me. Lockhardt was more resilient than we had planned for, and your friend wasn't good enough to be of use." Her words dripped with palpable disappointment.

"If we are going to assist one another, then you need to stop talking down on us. As useless as you might like to think we are, we got you here. You could be lying somewhere within the grasp of those goons right now, facing torture upon torture until you meet a slow death." Mike glared at her once more.

"We wouldn't even be here if my mission went properly," Lyssa replied smoothly before adding. "Or yours." Michael couldn't argue with that, but he didn't appreciate how she blamed part of her failure onto Hachi as well. Not when she wasn't there to defend herself.

He snatched up another dinner roll, tearing off a chunk with his thumb to pop into his mouth. He offered some to her, which she declined, so he pulled back.

"Where is your partner?" Lyssa asked, noticing that the ninja girl hadn't returned to the table yet.

"Probably sulking, I'm not sure. Why don't you go look? I'll handle the check." He stretched in his seat in the meantime as the fox stood up.

Outside, Hachi breathed fog into the night like cigarette smoke. She smirked at the novelty, trying it again, but it stopped there. Reciting the mantra she had made for herself, she sat cross-legged on the hood of Mike's sedan, blocking the outside world from her meditation. With Lockhardt at large, he would be much harder to assault. They had no clue where he would run to, and the red fox was sure to be shoring up his defenses. Right now, they would be hunting for him in vivid darkness, unless they could…by the slightest chance, lay their hands on more reliable and precise intel. They had to find him again, but starting at square one with no leads sounded like a bad prospect. Lockhardt hadn't known he was being stalked before but now it's different in that he knows, he would be more prepared next time.

Mike's connections had proven themselves inadequate so she will have to acquire info on her own for his safety's sake. That was only half of the problem. Oh, how nice it would be if Junior were still around. Having an accomplice in action would help her a lot, somebody to cover her blind spots and help take down foes. Somebody who, if he had been there these past few hours, would have helped finish off the red fox, especially after he had been wounded.

There was a tap on the glass. The girl who she had rescued stood by at a short distance. Hachi had calmed, but she noticed that the person outside the glass looked different from the one she left behind in the café.

Someone else. The ferret girl thought.

CHAPTER 5

The Heavenly Stone

Hachi carefully studied a map on the desk as she waited on Lyssa in a room nearby. The fox was checking her equipment right before they leave to pursue a new lead that they've uncovered. Since the previous night, the ferret couldn't help but feel some sympathy for the esper. The bandages wrapped around her head hid something that was not allowed to be revealed or else the attention it would draw would be an unwanted hindrance, according to the operative. The shinobi found Lyssa's mental powers rather impressive though. Versatile and highly potent. Plus, it turned out that her agency-backed resources were superior to Michael's meager info-gathering. Hachi sighed in relief because that means less running around completely blind for them.

"Are you good to go?" Hachi asked. The white fox raised her head as she stood, in higher spirits. Straightening her sleeves, Lyssa gave a thumbs up. For someone who doesn't speak much, seeing her new acquaintance smiling was a rare treat. Despite Lyssa's initial difficulty with interactions, the two managed to get along well enough now to be working together.

Hachi stashed the map back inside her pouch, making sure it was well out of sight as they exited the building and into the street. With their wits up, they trotted down the technology district where they passed crowds of figures, keeping to the shadows as often as possible.

The night was serene, quite unlike what they expected. The figures they were passing were all busy with one thing or another, giving the two ladies no trouble or attention. Smoke blew from a smoker's pipe beside an apartment building. As they continued on their way, they spoke no words to one another, taking care not to be conspicuous. Their mission needed stealth, given that Lockhardt could have a network of spies in play at his disposal. The esper skills came in handy. She kept a radius around them under telepathic surveillance, reading the minds of any hoodlums lurking in hidden spots. Hachi could see that it takes a bit of her to keep the field up. The ferret wished they didn't have to be so aware of everything around them. She helped too, using her keen senses to watch for sudden movements. Neither of them felt like they were being stalked, as the lack of footsteps showed them. It took a double take for them to ease off on the paranoia a bit.

While it probably wasn't optimal to deploy them together at once, it was their best bet to reach their goal. One backs the other up and there is no delay once they reach their location. Whatever lead they have now must not slip away from them, and that means being prepared to handle any surprises that may be lurking. The closer they got to their destination, the more eager they became for action. Just around the corner lingered a burnt down building, standing awkwardly in the dim light of the evening. Hachi had been eavesdropping on a recent buzz that involved private investigators hot on a sophisticated crime trail. By keeping their eyes open, the duo picked up enough clues to piece together where Lockhardt's next hideout was.

Apparently, rumors had surfaced about the shipment of nooscite that Lyssa had talked about prior. In the wrong hands, the meteorite could cause some serious havoc. After all, Lyssa herself was a result from experiments with that rock. Hachi wondered what would happen if someone found a way to optimize the effectiveness of the alien material better? It was something the private industry could afford, given they had the resources, along with a motive for it. A breakthrough would shift the wheel of power. The ninja girl quickly dismissed that worrying thought. Before anymore 'what if' questions popped inside her mind, like Lyssa planning to take the space crystals for her own gain, shook her head and decided to place her trust in the white fox. Fear brings out the worst in individuals, as the Takaro had seen it happen herself before.

One street turn later, the two made it to the blackened building. Hachi didn't hesitate to step right into the charred grounds. Her senses on high alert, she picked up the scent of two goons in the alley to the right. Both were canines. Without hesitation, Lyssa jumped ahead. Hachi wanted to tell her to wait a minute, but the fox had already disappeared behind the corner. The ferret quickly followed, slightly cursing to herself as she saw a couple of hoodlums about to aim their weapons' sights at them. The esper dove straight towards the nearest one.

Hachi leaped onto the left wall, springing off acrobatically before dropping down on the goon. He pulled the trigger too late. A round whizzed past the shinobi's ear as her heel made contact with his chest. "Oof!" He lost his grip on his gun and staggered but grabbed her foot in the process. With a swing, he slammed her to the wall behind him. Pain spread out from her back as she gritted her teeth to endure it. From the corner of her eye, Hachi watched Lyssa dealing with the other henchman, and from the looks of the fox's graceful movements, she has the situation under control.

Snapping back to her own fight, Hachi grabbed the henchman by his shoulders and used his own weight to scale herself up the wall once more so that she could escape and add some distance from him. The German shepherd stumbled backward and scrambled to regain his stance. Hachi used this opportunity to throw a jab at him, but he stepped back enough to avoid her by a slim margin. He aimed a slow kick at her gut, but the ferret merely stepped to the side to avoid it. He bounced from foot to foot, trying find an opening so he could launch his counterattack. Growing impatient, Hachi got serious. She intercepted his haymaker and swept her leg underneath him. As he fell, she struck the base of his neck, which shattered his collarbone. The dog yelped in pain, rolling over once on the ground before going into shock.

Lyssa's opponent was a not much luckier. She fought him quite unfairly, combining psychic combat with physical combat. Her movements were mystical, easing in and out with precise steps. The opponent sent her a straight kick, putting too much force into it, which the esper predicted easily. He lost his balance and began to fall. She kicked him back in return, sending him tumbling to the ground. He rolled over to stand up before his back had barely touched the ground, recovering well. The esper bullrushed him. Then, the hound aimed a blow at her temple. She hanged the fist mid-air with her mind, much to the canine's horror. Before he could register this, the esper kneed him in the lower abdomen. He doubled over, and the esper sent him back up with a carefully timed uppercut that took the air out of him. Staggered, and dazed, Lyssa went for the lockdown.

Hachi turned just in time to see Lyssa finish dispatching the other henchman. She watched as the esper placed him under a headlock, smiling to herself and the effectiveness of her methods while walking towards them.

"Where's the shipment?" Hachi interrogated him rather roughly. The brown mutt shook his head with his eyes shut. At this, she elbowed him in the gut, making him jerk forward and almost lose his lunch.

"Tell us about the nooscite now!"

"I-I don't know!" He sputtered out as Lyssa pulled him back up, letting her ears sit on behind her head. "There's a huge warehouse south of here. The boys there should know more."

There was no questioning the authenticity of the information. His confession from their painful interrogation was genuine as a hairlock. Hachi looked at Lyssa, and their eyes met. They had to pay a visit to this huge warehouse.

Finished with him, Lyssa flung the dog at a dumpster to the side. His face collided with the metal, knocking him out. Hachi gave a thankful nod at her partner. Most of this progress wouldn't have been possible in the first place without the esper's expansive resources. It was truly a great time-saver given the situation. And there was no time to waste either.

The two scaled up to the roof of the neighboring building to get a better view. Indeed, there was a warehouse down the street southbound. The esper held onto the ferret's hand as they jumped through the tops of the buildings, cheating a tad by using telekinesis. Hachi marveled at the feat, grateful that she doesn't have to expend her own energy for this lift. Once they got close enough, they hit the ground and snuck into an alley to the left. When Hachi peered out, she saw how huge the wooden building was in the still moonlight. Not just huge, it was likely well-guarded as well.

The place should have the information that they needed. "We should head to the office," Lyssa suggested. In Hachi's mind, that was a no-brainer, but the tricky part was finding it and getting past the guards. Of course, when they squinted through a window, the dark was crawling with shadows of hired thugs. The ferret sighed. It looks like they would be doing a lot of fighting if they couldn't find a way to take care of them all in one fell swoop. Four guards were stationed near the entrance, keeping watch. Two were cats, and the rest were possums. The Takaro wondered why these warriors wore nice suits when they must get into messy fights often. Another absurdity of this complex country, she thought.

First things first. Those guards by the door must be taken care of, in order to gain access inside. While it was easier said than done, these individuals proved to be not as difficult as Deltus or capable high-ranked ninja. Hachi's muscles twitched with desire for more action during the encounter. It started off with a fast exchange of blows, which Hachi dutifully dodged and blocked. Two against one, Hachi knew she shouldn't keep that up given the fight to come. She kicked one of the cats in the chest, sending him flying backward to the walls. While he struggled for composure, she returned to the other kitty. The cat introduced weapons, brandishing a knife quite suddenly. Her foe flailed to slice her with his knife, but in a casual fashion, she fractured his leg with a well-timed kick. The crack of his bones was audible as he clutched his limb in agony. He was done for, Hachi left him just as the other feline came charging.

Another one down with more to follow. She thought to herself.

Meanwhile, Lyssa was not slacking off. Jumping at one of the possums, the esper struck him in the back of his neck, knocking him out. His partner fired a silenced gun in her direction. Expecting such an attack, Lyssa combined a force field with evasive movements to deflect the two rounds, which ricocheted away safely. He rolled away, ducked and expelled another barrage of bullets at the esper. Again, she cast a force field to fend them off. The gunman sensed foul play so he improvised, coming at her with a flying kick. Lyssa knew it was a feint. He was obviously trying to get in close for a point blank shot. Without letting her guard down, Lyssa parried his kick and yanked him down to the floor. He landed harshly and tried standing up fast. The white fox wasted no time in stopping him from catching his breath. Using full force, the white fox jabbed his stomach. He stumbled back and dropped his firearm. Then, she finished him off with a kick to the throat. He groaned as he slumped, down for the count. Taking in a deep breath, the fox surveyed how Hachi was doing.

The ferret was untouchable to the feline's swipes. He threw two quick jabs at her in succession. She dodged them both, shifting her body swiftly from side to side. The himalayan was mad with fury. He came at Hachi recklessly. The Takaro likes these types of situations. It gave her the opportunity to finish him quickly. Dodging his flurry of attacks, Hachi found an opening among her surroundings. She positioned their fight so that when the ninja hopped above him, the guard tripped and fell down. Of course, this allowed the shinobi to land a heel on his skull. Even before he landed, she knew that kitty was not recovering from that tonight.

Once they were through taking them out, they approached the door stealthily. Opening it gingerly without as much as a creaking sound, they peeped in first, not to take in the interior but to look out for any thugs lurking near. Seeing none, they entered the warehouse and hid behind a crate so that they could better get a lay of the land that they would be dealing with.

The inside was more spacious than what it looked like from outside. Stairways led to higher levels and offices behind doors scattered around the building. A loading area was also present in the back of the facility. The females stuck to the shadows as they searched for the head office, which they would be able to pinpoint since it's likely under heavy guard. The Takaro hoped that the mafioso boss was not there. That would be more trouble for them, if the mission did not go according to plan a second time. After scouting a number of henchman in various posts, Lyssa then gently tapped her on the shoulder. The white fox brought Hachi to higher ground quietly to check a large door on the upper level. It was under careful watch by two lions, their hands behind their backs. They gave off an aura that the mooks the two have faced so far lacked. Hachi deduced that they must have formal training in close quarters combat and are protecting the office that they're after.

Hachi could see a clear path to the door. However, if they caused too much noise, it would attract the rest of the goons' attention. Of course, while they could always just take out the whole warehouse, that would be highly inefficient, and there had to be at least twenty, if not more, henchman. A different approach should be devised.

Hachi felt the adrenaline within her from taking out the outside guards making the ferret's tail twitch wildly behind her. Lyssa huffed beside her, a bit tense since the elite guards noticed something and started walking towards their hiding place.

Lyssa pulled the ferret close and spoke to her. "I'm going to cover the vicinity with a sound barrier, so you need to take those two out while I concentrate. Got it?"

Hachi watched her set to work, the muscles around her temples tensing and relaxing. She concentrated hard. The purple in her eyes glowed mildly as her eyeballs stood still. Her body went still as she set her eyes in the direction of the thugs. Through gritted teeth, she looked briefly at her partner and mouthed a 'now'.

Hachi nodded before springing into action, leaping to the top of the box and shocking the lions. Getting in front of one of them, the shinobi started with a fan kick. It missed though as the brute jumped back in time, displaying his athletics. Hachi wanted to push them away from Lyssa, so she lunged forward franticly to grasp at the closest one's neck. Bad move!

The big cat brought his legs up and kicked Hachi's stomach in midair, pushing the ferret backward as pain flared in the center of her body. Coughing a bit, she pulled herself up and corrected her footing as the other lion rushed at her. Hachi watched as a barrel fell on top of the henchman, it seems that Lyssa is still able to provide some support while maintaining her barrier. The Takaro dropkicked the dazed barrel lion, which made it, roll fast, prompting the first cat to jump over it. Hachi swayed to the side of the railing. With a smirk, she beckoned the other guard to come at her.

He did so, and the shinobi used his momentum to catch and flip him over the railing. The elite's fall would have caused a ruckus but he caught the bottom of the walkway just in time. Hachi saw that he had a difficult choice—either he stayed there or lose his grasp and fall. As this was going on, the second lion removed the barrel and went back to aid his partner. Around this time, Lyssa choked out to Hachi. "You need to hurry up, I don't know how much longer I can keep the sound suppressed!"

Hachi nodded and took out a kunai, which she used to impale one of the guard's hands while she used the white fox's handcuff to fasten his other hand to the railing. Just to be extra sure, she shut his pained yelling up with a mouth gag carried by the ninja girl. "Quiet, you." She chided.

The remaining brute growled, his claws out and his mane flared up. The ferret saw her partner struggling so she resolved to end this without playing around now that it was one-on-one. She yanked the kunai out of the still bleeding paw, which made the hapless cat recoil as blood stained his long sleeves. In one swift motion, she dashed under the mad lion and slashed his neck open. It was not an exchange. It was a massacre. At that moment, the white fox saw her friend's killing potential in her yellow eyes.

Unable to speak out, the elite guard expired in front of them as the other swung inches from death by his bonds. Lyssa finally relaxed and dispelled the sound barrier. Now that the threats were subdued, the fox and ferret made their way into the management's office. They do not know when the goons below will suspect something up where they were so it is now a race with the clock.

Thinking fast, Hachi pushed a small cabinet in the room in front of the door so that it would buy them some extra time should they need it when rummaging through the room. Papers were scattered all over the desk at the far end of the room. It was vacant when they entered it.

"This is great, the intel here is just what we need!" Hachi exclaimed joyfully as her hands sifted through the papers. After putting up with disappointment for the past few days, things started to look up for once. Shipment dates, routes and the like. When Lyssa saw it for herself, she couldn't help but breathe easier. Gathering the stack of documents in a knapsack bag, Hachi continued to scour the place, this time for other useful items such as evidence or important equipment. "When we find your meteorite, we find Benjamin."

Kicking down a locker, it seemed that they've found a modest weapons cache. None of which that Hachi would practically use. She found the foreign tools too bulky for her style, and she barely understood the mechanisms of operating them even. Lyssa called for her and asked for the bag. "Let me hold onto that for you."

The ferret complied and gave it to the fox girl. "Thanks, Lyssa.

Keep them safe until we get out of here." With that said, they completed their search and left the room. As they passed the defeated lions and went down the stairs, the warehouse felt deathly silent. Alarm bells sounded in the ninja's head. Is this an ambush?

Warning Lyssa, they paused at the middle of the stairs and looked towards the ground floor below them. There looked to be an aged possum down there. Hachi had to squint as she watched him bark orders to some henchmen. His style of dress was oddly different compared to everyone she met, including the esper. The snow fox held the papers tightly as if they meant everything to her. His ears suddenly perked and their senses picked up a rancid stench in the air. The two had to cover their noses for several moments as the old marsupial suddenly looked up at them. Raising a brow, the ferret girl took herself back. There was evil behind his strange mask.

Without warning, there was a sudden crashing noise and heat spiked up on the metal surface where the ladies stood. Hachi hissed in pain coming from a mild burning on the soles of her feet. The stairs gave way and the both of them came crashing down to the ground floor. Dust flew around them from the impact as the Takaro found herself choking on the putrid air. Realization hit them both. Their activities must have been noticed while they were in the manager's office and the strange possum must have planted whatever melted the stairs. Her instincts made her look for Lyssa, her eyes catching the fox. She was disorientated but otherwise still in one piece. The shinobi's momentary ease disappeared when she saw the enemy not too far in front of her.

The Takaro felt her body tense, looking up she finally got to see this newcomer face to face. He had some strange weapons attached to his belt. A brown costume adorned with all sorts of mysterious cogs and quirks. His black mask covered his entire head and neck; his eyes covered by thick round lenses. As he stood with his arms crossed, Hachi found herself reflexively holding her breath. She forced some distance between them by hopping at least two yards back as the possum stared at her with his icy disposition.

"The name's Chemisteer." He introduced himself as Lyssa stood up. The intel bag was missing but the fox went to Hachi's side seeing as there was a bigger issue at the moment. She scowled at the possum. Her mind probing wasn't having much effect on him for some reason. His either must be well-tempered or his mind was abnormal. "My job is to get rid of pests like you ladies."

Hachi tapped Lyssa's shoulder to snap her back to the present. One way or another, they were going to get past this so called 'Chemisteer'.

CHAPTER 6

Rogue Freelancer

The current situation looked grim. The geezer stepped forward, armor and weaponry rustling all about him, while Hachi watched anxiously. Nearby, some goons inside the warehouse were handling some boxes, no doubt carrying out criminal operations, but all Lyssa and Hachi could do was stand and watch. The possum leered, then drew a rifle-shaped apparatus. Attached to it was a canister etched with a symbol and some text that Lyssa could just barely make out. Her eyes widened when she identified it. Even before Lyssa told her what it was, Hachi got the memo to avoid it no matter what.

"Cyclone D. For pest removal," Lyssa stated plainly.

So that's what it was. The shinobi mentally scolded herself for leaving her golden wakizashis behind. Their wind powers would've certainly helped them out in this particular bind. It didn't look like she'd be able to rely on Lyssa either. Fighting their way inside the building took a lot of energy out of the white fox, and she was still trying to conserve her reserves. That sound field earlier was no joke on the esper's exertion. Hachi was still analyzing the rather disadvantageous situation when the Chemisteer spoke once more.

"You ladies must be after this shipment behind me, aren't you?" He jabbed his thumb backwards over his shoulder. Right behind him stood an armored truck, parked as henchmen loaded items in and out of the vehicle. Hachi scowled. Their objective was right there in front of them, yet still, one more obstacle stood in their way. It was tempting just to rush in boldly anyway and bypass that one final hazard. But she knew that that would be both stupid and dangerous.

"Where do you plan on sending that?" Hachi asked the marsupial who kept a close watch. "Do you even know what you are dealing with?"

"I suppose I've got time to kill..." His tone dripped with an air of condescendence. He laughed mischievously, seeming to be enjoying the situation. "That right there's a powerful source of energy. The profit potential is beyond the likes of your comprehension." Shrugging his shoulders, he shook his head smugly. "If you think I will tell you where it's headed, then you are dumber than I thought."

The Takaro was slightly on edge, nervous. She took a couple of deep breaths to calm herself down, but from the corner of her vision, she saw Lyssa already making her move. She decided to keep the conversation going, as a form of distraction.

 "I don't suppose you'd tell us that. I was just checking to be sure you know the consequences of your actions." He probably wasn't a moralist, but she couldn't think of anything better to say. It seemed to be working as he responded to her, not watching as Lyssa kept planning her starting move.

"You bet," he replied with a crooked smile. "If it pays good money, then it's good business. I don't-"

The esper dashed for the armored vehicle despite the danger. It all happened in a flash, catching the marsupial in mid-speech. Retrieving the nooscite ASAP was the esper's primary objective after all. This forced Hachi to flank the possum early. However, he reacted by unleashing a cloud of toxic gas in their direction. Lyssa suddenly found herself at the front of the attack, caught by surprise. She inhaled the gas. The smoke was choking, making her to cough. Hachi thought quickly, then scanned her surroundings, spotting a gas mask laying on the floor. She was far enough from the cloud to snatch it up and slip it over her face, just in time. It took a moment for her eyes to adjust, but the mask did its job in safeguarding her from the poison. Lyssa wasn't so fortunate, and she was soon coughing in the substance and gasping for breath. Without any way to shield herself, the esper was quickly inundated by the poison.

Before the fox's exposure could grow even worse, Hachi grabbed Lyssa and boosted her up to one of the rafters above safely. She set the fox down and checked on her partner's status. Lyssa fought the effects of the chemical, nodding reassuringly. She tried to sit up with pretentious agility. "Sorry, I can...still fight." Hachi knew she was only trying to sound assuring. The poison was nonetheless having its effect take hold.

"Lyssa, you're going to be okay. Just save your energy. We'll get the nooscite back." Their exchange was cut short by a shell whizzing past their heads and detonating, releasing more gas. The two split up in different directions for evasive action. They couldn't afford to lose that truck this evening. Of course, Lyssa couldn't handle taking in more of the poisonous gas either.

Hanging underneath a stairway, Hachi peeked to see what the possum was up to. For his age, he doesn't appear bogged down by his equipment. His reflexes were also in good condition since he spotted her not long after. He twirled round towards and launched another gaseous attack, all within the blink of an eye. A burst of green acid followed and eroded the metal she was holding on to almost instantly. She dropped down to the beam below her and then narrowed her gaze. He was starting to tick her off. If she didn't find a way to defeat him soon, the toxin in Lyssa's veins would eventually kill her.

The ferret ran across the beam, dodging the acid shots flying past her. She could feel the heat emanating off of them as they barely grazed her body. She circled in evasion, making sure to stay within his sight but far out enough to make his aiming difficult. It was a technique meant to do two things—force him to waste his supply and also close the gap between them without being scorched by the acid. She jumped down and swung her heel out at the Chemisteer, relying more on luck than certain calculation. It was difficult seeing her target, and consequentially, aiming through the less than clear lenses of the gas-mask, and as expected, the Chemisteer easily sidestepped her attack. He immediately countered, grabbing her ankle with his tail and flinging her away from him. Then he followed up with his gun, lining up the sight in the wake of her airborne body. As Hachi barrelled through the air, she saw parts of the floor steaming with corrosive acid.

Lyssa snuck behind on the railing, trying her own pre-emptive attack. The Takaro hoped that the white fox would get a better chance since he was preoccupied with her at the time. To give the esper more chance, the ferret girl kept at the bald tail, tempting him to keep wasting his ammo on a moving target.

Lyssa leaped from the railing, aiming to strike at his blind spot. She felt winded. A simple breath met a burning sensation each time. But her tempered determination was what kept her from keeling over. He turned toward her just before her fist would connect. It landed on his armored shoulder, causing him to drop his weapon. Then, the esper backflipped away as he reached for the sidearm on his belt. It shot a dart which nearly hit the fox's arm, making her fur stand on end. Her instincts and powers flashed briefly. With her ears twitching, she noticed a few vials strapped to his vest, one of them looked particularly odd. The antidote must be on his person.

Gears started to turn inside the vulpine's head. Chemisteer steadied his aim, pointing his pistol right between her violet eyes. "Nice try, but it's going to take more than that to faze me." He scoffed before he fired again.

Lyssa flinched, stationary for all shooting purpose, too stunned by the burning sensation within her to move, but Hachi got in front of her, deflecting the dart with a well-timed kunai. Her eyes had finally managed to adjust to the mask. She threw her knife squarely at the possum's hand, knocking the gun right out of it. Disarmed, he began to step back slowly in retreat. Before the females could go after him, two gorillas jumped from the shadows blockading them from the possum. He sneered while Lyssa slumped over, trying to resist the poison's effects with great effort. "He has...the antidote!" she choked in what was a loud, laborious whisper.

"Have fun playing with those primates, girls." Chemisteer fell back, disappearing from their sight.

Hachi grimaced, she needed to snag that antidote and treat her friend quick. She couldn't live with another death on her conscience.

First things first, the overgrown monkeys need to be put down. Drawing from her inner *qi*, Hachi grabbed Lyssa to get her out of harm's way from the incoming henchmen. The esper closed her eyes and overrode her body's aspiratory reflexes with her powers, nodding in thanks. It was a trade-off. It took all her psychic power and thus completely shut off her access to any psychic ability, but it delayed the poison's effects, giving them precious time to act. Hachi noticed this change in her partner and was impressed by her versatility. That meteorite must mean a lot to someone such as Lyssa.

For now, the shinobi will have to make do with less weaponry on hand. Without a doubt, their opponents' sizes may prove troublesome. As they charged toward the girls, Hachi and Lyssa were steadily getting pushed back, unable to advance. Soon, they found themselves in an area surrounded by debris. Around them were various broken pipes, glass shards, and other assorted trash.

"Trust me Hachi; I'll be fine on my own," Lyssa told the ninja girl. Hachi sighed, and the two split up once more to commence their counterattack.

The ferret checked her surroundings for anything that she could use to her advantage. She wasn't going to rely on blind luck to bail her out against those meatheads. There were a lot of boxes inside the building with items within them. Normally, she would be more thorough but time was of the essence. A quick and crude strategy would make do.

Picking up a broken pipe from the floor, Hachi turned towards a gorilla and assumed a kendo stance. The thug grew wary and kept his distance. She gave him an intimidating gaze before assaulting him with the metal object and striking him multiple times, littering his body in welts.

   CLANG! *CLANG!*

The ape staggered, trying to block her blows with his large arms but she danced around him and kept up her assault. He stepped back, and Hachi advanced, drumming the pipe all over his body. The ape, sensing his blocks did not affect rather affording him a swelling hand, let go off his guards in a bit to launch an attack. The shinobi feinted a low pipe hit, dropping so that his outstretched blow whisked over the vacuum above her head. The move exposed his nape, which she capitalized on. In a flurry, she got up and harnessing all her might, jumping and landing a critical hit to the exposed nape which caused him to collapse onto the floor.

The ninja looked to see how well her fox partner was faring. Unsurprisingly, she was having some difficulty. Her usual powers were not active which reduced her combat ability. Lyssa got distracted for a moment and got caught by the gorilla by her tail. Hachi dashed on ahead right away to help out, sending a spinning kick to the brute's hand, which forced him to let go. Then, she used her metal pipe to thwack him hard on his forehead. The thug flailed his arm and swatted Hachi to the wall before she was about to finish him off. *THUD!* The impact stunned her. He was not finished as he followed her flailing body, hoping to pin her to the wall with his knees. Lyssa managed to yank Hachi away before he could pound her to the ground.

Regaining her senses, Hachi saw the goon scrambling towards her with a threatening snarl. She predicted his movements and jumped up, delivering a knee to his abdomen. This made him stumble backward in pain while clutching his gut. It was the perfect chance for a finishing move, but the ape had reflexes.

The shinobi raised her pipe once more, and the gorilla attempted to catch it in mid-air. She faked out at the last second, twisting it and hitting him squarely on the shoulder. It gave an audible crack.

Lyssa followed up with a surprise chokehold from behind him. Using a double arm lock, the white fox intended to knock out him out fast. With Hachi's swordplay assisting her, he was unable to pry her arms from his neck. The esper looked annoyed that she was needing help, thanks to her poisoned state. It was hard to breathe normally, and her muscles felt increasing more like lead. She growled as he fumbled backwards and pressed her to the wall to make her release him. The pain was subtle at first but morphed within seconds into something excruciating. She let go of her arm lock.

With Lyssa finally letting go, Hachi put him down with a well-placed strike. He slinked facedown first and was no longer a threat. Both high threat bodyguards were now out of commission.

The two made their way back to the armored truck, watching for any traps that the marsupial might have set. They found none yet unexpectedly, he hopped onto them from somewhere above them. The two went for him immediately but taking extra care this time. He pulled out his blaster in response. The ferret was keeping an eye on Lyssa for any more complications. If Hachi had to kill him for the antidote, then she would.

Adjusting her gas mask, Hachi pressed the attack as soon as Chemisteer showed an opening. The fox's pace was being slowed down by her coughing. Hachi slipped behind the possum before he could tag her with his corrosive acid. His suit proved resistant against her melee attacks though. It's of high quality despite the antiquated style. The kunoichi wondered what else could work. She was not about to give up. Not tonight.

"I must give you girls credit really, you're making my evening more interesting than usual." He shifted more of his attention to Hachi for defense since the fox was handicapped. "You're not smart though...taking on a poison user and getting exposed. How foolish. Your friend is obstinate by staying conscious too!" He gestured towards Lyssa, much to Hachi's annoyance. She grew irritated with his jabs.

"You will eat those words!" She took out her dagger to stab him, but Chemisteer distanced himself while she wasn't paying attention. The old possum shifted to a pile of crates nearby, making the two narrow their eyes. Just as Lyssa and Hachi thought, he was using some sort of drug to enhance his physical capabilities.

The duo saw a shift in the henchmen transferring goods to the vehicles. Their thinning numbers indicated that the operation was almost complete. Some had already entered their cars and drove off ahead of the rest. Slicing a rope with the weight hanging from the ceiling, she held the hold, and as the weight went crashing down, it drew her rope up quickly to the Chemisteer's level. She prepared to continue their brawl.

She pursued the mercenary once more, avoiding shells and acid, which she had gotten used to now. With Lyssa out of range, it was all up to Hachi now to dispose of this poisoner. Meanwhile, Lyssa sneaked out of sight and attached a small device with an antenna onto the armored truck. "Just in case..." Lyssa whispered to herself. If they could not stop the shipment, then they would track it for later.

Chemisteer clicked his tongue as he continued to shoot at Hachi. She made dodging them look easy, but one mistake could mean death, so the pressure was on all the same. The gas mask wouldn't stop acid, after all. Hachi slashed at him after getting within range. She knew she had made a hit as the poisoner face contorted with pain. He stepped back, starting to sweat a bit. She is not letting him escape this time. She had to get the antidote somehow, Lyssa's life depended on it.

Back on the ground, Lyssa had hidden from sight in the vents below to avoid getting into more unwanted scuffles. The venom was taking its toll, in that her powers were starting to be overwhelmed fighting its detrimental effects. Right now, she needed medical attention and to reserve her strength. Lyssa reached into her shirt pocket, pulling out a communicator and speaking to it.

"Michael...requesting pick-up soon...I'm not...feeling well."

Back on the stacks of crates, Chemisteer appeared hesitant on using his acid gun at close quarters. Hachi noticed this and grinned within her mask. The playing field was more level when removing his range advantage. The possum also had to watch his step carefully, lest he falls off from that considerable height. Around him, the crates lacked railing. The tide seemed to favor Hachi from now on; if this kept up, then she might be able to get some good hits in. Yet, he made a quick, precise movement, seeking to put space between them again so he could once again make use of the acid gun. Hachi knew better than to allow this, closing every space before he had even opened them.

Eventually, he slowed down enough so that in a few quick motions, she cut his suit in several places. It was what Hachi had anticipated. The shinobi was trying to get a feel of his weak points and saw that she drew blood in the stomach area. Not so much the others. In a few seconds, Hachi thought of the best way to kill him. While she only knew Lyssa for a day, she would never forgive the underhanded, sadistic tactics of Chemisteer.

TSSS!

The look on his face revealed tension, and now he was taking risks to get rid of her as he aimed close to his body with her needing to roll to the side to avoid his sizzling chemicals.

Landing near the edge, Hachi went behind some cover to get away from his sight. She has got him on the ropes now, so all she needs is to ambush him when he least expects it. The Chemisteer went for his sidearm for extra measure. He lacked support from his underlings and lost sight of that ninja. He gripped his weapons tightly, beads of sweat perspiring down his furred face. He knew the fight had changed but what he didn't know, was that he shouldn't be panicking. That was exactly what the shinobi wanted—for him to panic. Lunging forward from the shadows, she managed to tackle him and plummet them both back to the ground floor. He was stunned in midair, dropping his weapons as she made him take the brunt of the impact with a loud thud. Suit or not, Hachi knew the fall would do him in, if not altogether kill him.

From that bold move, Hachi crawled away from the lying possum and slowly got back up, panting. She looked at him and thought for sure he was done for, but after several moments, he groaned and began to move his muscles under his suit. His foolish cat seemed to have more than nine lives.

"Impossible." She was taken aback by his unnatural durability. Was he a freak like her partner was too?

"Black market steroids, little ferret!" He scoffed as he pulled himself together, coughing once or twice. His mask was damaged, and his eyeholes showed his aged visage which seethed maliciously. It was similar but not quite the same as the dark one's influence on Tekiya.

Lyssa threw one last gaze at the armored vehicle from her hiding spot. It was about to take off, and the fox could only watch as her meteorites go out of reach. Cursing herself silently, the esper collapsed from the stress on her body. Somehow, it felt to her like yet another failure.

Hachi acknowledged that this foe must have been much more deadly in his prime, but right now he was old; she could handle this. While he ran to snatch his weapons, she closed their distance and reached him just as soon as his hand grabbed his rifle. The possum was about to shoot at her, his gear shifting rather audibly. That suit must have weighed considerably heavy, yet his enhancements allowed him to move in a way that impressed the ferret. The round grazed her as she tried to evade it, making her hiss. Her dagger slashed into his shoulder making him growl with pain. He dropped his weapon once more, and with it, his means to victory.

The shinobi finished him off with a full power elbow to his head, and that was lights-out for him. Crumbling to the floor, Hachi scrambled up to him to rummage through his jacket. The white vial was there, and she grabbed it, taking the rest, as much as she can, for a backup. Then, Hachi rushed over to Lyssa. Picking up the fox's body delicately, Hachi checked her vital signs to see if there is still a response. Lyssa's pulse seemed faint. All of the henchmen had vacated by now, and a siren could be heard from the distance. The few intel they managed to scrounge up and the tracker Lyssa planted on the truck were their last hope. But at that moment, the Takaro was preoccupied with the drive to treat her friend as soon as possible, and she left the area to meet back with Michael on their getaway car.

Even as she raced to him, she was waving for him to come, her arms flailing wildly in the air. Michael knew immediately that she needed help with Lyssa, she didn't sound too good on the distress call. He put shifted gears, turning the steering frantically to steer the car to back the oncoming ferret. For a moment, Hachi thought he was leaving them. Then, he went into reverse. Hachi saw what he was doing then. She stopped approaching the car and ran back to Lyssa. Before she was back with her, Mike had parked the car and shot out towards them. Between them, they carried the white fox to the car and got in, Hachi getting in the back with the white fox.

While Michael drove at breakneck speed away from the warehouse as far as possible, Hachi busied herself with reviving the esper. She broke the antidote tube and held it slowly at the esper's nose. Even in her dizzy state, she could feel her throat choke again as the antidote's effects sneaked in. She writhed in pain, in response to a reaction that must be going on within her veins, the antidote doing its work. Hachi held the tube to her nose again, giving her more doses of the antidote to inhale. Perspiration broke from the operative's body. "Is she dying Michael?!"

Michael looked from the rearview mirror and saw the convulsing esper. He knew she was not dying but reacting to drugs fighting through her system. Reassuring Hachi that she would be okay, he darted his gaze back to the road just as a greyish saber-frill jumped on the road out of nowhere. He swerved as the tires streaked, leaving a thick cloud of smoke in their wake. Michael cursed, muttering under his breath.

The ferret girl watched as the white fox began to relax, her attention away from their near accident, even though it had just jolted her harshly. The esper finally relaxed and lost consciousness.

CHAPTER 7

Downtime

A full day had passed. Yet still, Hachi couldn't stop thinking about what happened the night before. The warehouse operation had been going relatively smoothly until the Chemisteer showed up, more like until they bumped into him. For all they know, he could have been at the warehouse all day. The events of last night played through her head on loop throughout practice, punctuated by the mechanical sword strikes she took out on the wooden dummy in front of her. She vented her frustration and stress on the dummy, hitting it hard with her *bokken* every time she struck.

They were all staying back at Michael's loft, one of their safe houses, as they waited out the storm. Lyssa had been bedridden ever since they arrived, all the while the salaryman was doing his best to nurse her back to health. It had taken her a while to recover since she had a high fever but he had been there for her, lowering her temperature with a cold towel and bottle of painkillers. Hachi pondered how the situation would have been different with Junior. Perhaps it would have not mattered much, but she knew that Michael could also do things that he couldn't. It had become apparent that this mission needed more than just fighting skills. Michael happened to fill those requirements in spades.

They had time to rest as long as the tracker performed its task well. The armored vehicle had made several stops so far, none appeared to be the final destination, and there were likely still several more ahead. Hachi felt restless, but she thought back to her sensei's fervent teachings on the virtue of patience and re-steeled her resolve. Despite all of these setbacks in this new land, the ability to keep one's composure and wait for an opportunity is key to a mission's success. She needed Lyssa to get well soon, her extra hands had proven to be highly reliable thus far.

She intensified her blows, seeing the goons where the dummy stood. Breaking away sweat upon sweat, she swung the wooden stick here and there, hitting the dummy in different targeted areas with a preciseness that testified to her long hours of fervent training. She must be prepared for their next outing. The opponents she has faced so far proved not to be mere push-offs.

The ferret let out a sigh, stepping back and putting away her *bokken*. It was almost noon now so she might as well check up on Lyssa to see if her condition had improved. Her fever last night was particularly nasty. While the antidote cured her of any immediate danger, there was still some residual poison that had to make its way out of her system, much to her chagrin. Perhaps if Lyssa could take a walk or get some sunshine, it might hasten her recovery, Hachi thought. She entered the glass doorway, then turned right and went down the hallway. She stopped in front of the room where the white fox spent the night. Hachi paused as Michael walked past her, carrying a steaming bowl of soup on a food tray.

"Ah, how's it going Hachi? I brought this for our friend." The steam wafting from the soup carried with it a smell that was quite appetizing. Hachi raised her brow for a moment on the mention of the word 'friend' but let it pass as she expected nothing less from one of the male ferret's expertly prepared meals. He gave the door a polite knock before entering. The white fox was sitting up on her bed, rubbing her eyes a little. She definitely looked better than before, aside from the obvious lethargy. Since getting her partner back in action was of utmost importance, Hachi took the tray from Michael and asked him to give them some privacy, thanking him before approaching her friend.

"I'll leave you to it then." He said, exiting the room.

"Thank you." She replied.

Hachi sat beside Lyssa's bedside on a blue armchair. The esper accepted the tray and began to sip her soup while the Takaro watched, flicking her tail to one side as she observed her every action. It was remarkable to see the fox powering through her condition. Such dedication to the mission is worthy of a warrior's respect. The shinobi was grateful to have someone like her helping out in this job. After clearing her throat, Lyssa voiced her own gratitude.

"You have my thanks, Hachi." Lyssa moved her purple gaze towards Hachi thoughtfully. It took the other by surprise as she softened up. "I-I would…probably be dead without your help." The ferret bashfully rubbed the back of her head in response. All she did was standard procedure really, nothing special, she thought. Lyssa was essential to the operation after all. Losing her would deal a grave blow to acquiring their only lead regarding the Dark One.

"Ah, don't worry about it! I need you well and alive, you see," she quickly explained. Not only that, but Lyssa was also the key to so many resources that basically made their success so far. It was a partnership forged by necessity, certainly, but wouldn't it be wasteful not also to relax while there is time available? Hachi felt another driving force behind helping the fox, a more personal one. She found that she had started to empathize with Lyssa, the issues she had to deal with, they touched her. Hence, the shinobi's desire to give Lyssa a brief respite that she has earned.

It was then that Hachi smiled curtly and raised a finger as Lyssa put down her empty tray. "Say...now that you're done with brunch, why don't we take a walk in the park? It's not far from here, and we could use some fresh air." She made a convincing wide smile, trying as much to sound innocent.

Lyssa's ears twitched at the ferret's suggestion. It sounded ridiculous coming from the foreigner but to be honest, it had been too long since she had taken a stroll in daylight.

"There's no need-", the fox tried to object, but to no avail. Hachi wasn't having any of it.

"Aww, come on!" the ferret pleaded, nearly getting on Lyssa's nerves. "It will be good for you, I promise."

"...Fine," she relented. It was futile arguing with the ninja girl. Hachi beamed upon her victory over this matter.

She picked up the empty dishes and left, leaving Lyssa to herself. Putting on some inconspicuous civilian clothes, Hachi waited near the main entrance for the fox to get ready. Of course, she informed Michael, who was cleaning the safehouse, about their day out.

"That sounds like a great idea. I will stay here though. Have fun you two." He pulled out some spending money and handed it to the female ferret.

Crossing her arms, she huffed and shook her head jokingly. She felt bad taking his pocket change, but he insisted. Today is their holiday, and they should enjoy it while they can. Michael has definitely earned some alone time from constantly babysitting them. As she left, Hachi briefly glanced down at the bandages covering up where she'd been scraped but was satisfied with their inconspicuous appearance.

Several minutes later, Lyssa came down the hallway. She looked totally different in something other than her work clothes—she actually looked pretty nice. She had on a casual blouse set and fresh wrappings to replace the old ones. She met with Hachi and nodded that she was ready to get going. As the ferret girl opened the door, Lyssa stepped out and took a deep breath of the fresh air. Clouds that populated the sky passed them by like slow cotton. She went beside Hachi, starting their trek.

The nice cool air descended on the two briefly, its natural crispness felt pleasant to the touch. Breathing it in was like a mild form of aromatherapy, Hachi couldn't tell who needed it more, the fox next to her or herself. It was a taste of nature was needed for the weary fighters. Somehow, it felt right to have dragged the Lyssa out for this day at the park. At least, it was nice to see luster rushing back to both of their furs.

The park they were headed to wasn't grand or anything like that, but it still had ample space with trees scattered on the sides of their winding paths. "I've never spent time with nature as much ever since becoming an esper," Lyssa admitted as her steps rustled the fallen leaves on the pavement. Hachi figured as much. On the other hand, the ferret had a different upbringing. She had been raised near nature back in her homeland. It was all this new technology that she didn't quite understand.

"You know, I was used to seeing beautiful trees every day I went out. Though this country is fine in its own ways as well." The sky was overcast, and the wind was gentle, so the weather was pleasant. Hachi chuckled as they turned a corner and arrived at park's gate. A large sign placed on an overhead arch told the name of the park as Hachi and Lyssa went in. Thankfully, it was not a busy time when children could be seen filling the park. There were not too many people present. The Takaro loved such emptiness, the last thing she would want for their outing is for it to be ruined by constant wailing of some overgrown babies or unruly brats.

Hachi felt energized. With renewed vigor, the ferret jogged into the open field and somersaulted onto it. Lyssa followed behind, watching in confusion. The ninja girl laid on the grass with a satisfied smirk. When the ferret invited the fox to join her on the lawn, the esper refused, shaking her head. "What's wrong? Scared of a little dirt?" Hachi teased which made the fox turn away coldly.

Feeling slightly mischievous, the ferret tackled the esper. Wrapping her arms around the other's waist, the ferret girl brought her down next to her on the soft grass. As Lyssa tumbled, her fur puffed and got unkempt like Hachi's. She could feel the tenseness in her partner's movements. *Looks like somebody is wound up tight.* She thought.

"Bu-hey! Why the heck did you push me?" Lyssa quickly sat back up, her ears twitching as she took a few steps back. Hachi stuck her tongue out playfully at the wincing fox. The scene was idyllic. Park-goers passed them by on the long path that went around the park, occasionally throwing random glances. A pond was placed in the center of a landscape dotted with grassy hills. There was a hiking trail, on one side, that went into a small cave. Hachi felt more at ease here than she realized. It evoked a certain nostalgic feeling within her. She missed her old home, but in order to get back, she needed to focus on advancing this important mission of theirs.

Hachi took a moment to listen to the pteros as they flew in the branches, ignoring Lyssa's fussing. "Relax...nobody is going to attack us here in broad daylight." The ferret reassured the other girl. Taking the cue, Lyssa made an effort by sitting back down on the field and dusting off her tail, returning its former sheen.

The silver fox sighed and rested her hands behind her. Hachi gave her a gentle nudge.

"See? Pretty calm now." The ferret stretched casually. Lyssa's pulse gradually slowed down, her head clearing up as well. This might be the only opportunity they have for a real breather before the tracker results inevitably whisk them back into action. She began to feel the relevance of their outing. The sensation was similar to meditation but much more holistic as it was enjoyable along with relaxing. She stretched out some more, mimicking the posture of the shinobi. The esper could see the euphoria lining on her partner's face. She could tell that this ferret was as hard of a slacker as she handled serious business.

"So, you used to do this often?" Lyssa asked Hachi. She wasn't normally the type to go delving into someone else's past, but the ninja nodded back anyway.

"I used to play outside with my brother all the time where we once lived." She replied, breaking her smile for a second. Lyssa sensed that Hachi wasn't going to share much more than that. She felt it impolite to pry on one's affairs if all it did was bring back somber memories. The white fox leaned back and stared at the sky, taking in the blue horizon mixed with white clouds. The ferret girl's light humming, together with the stillness of nature, washed away Lyssa's stressors.

It was beautiful. Now that she could feel it, Lyssa felt a tugging at her heart that missed this experience. Life for her had been mostly going through motions since volunteering for the Nooscite project. Fresh air or even the outside became only part of her missions. Whatever time she was not on a mission, she was indoors, risking being seen by outsiders. Sometimes, she practices, honing her skills some more. Still, those didn't compare to what she was feeling right now. The aura in the daytime was welcoming, and the scenery around was fascinating with alluring flowers all over the place.

"I've never really taken the time to appreciate being outside like this before; it's nice." She noted to Hachi, who appeared to be deep in thought. "I feel better, and my aches aren't as bad as before..." The Takaro's rounded ears twitched as an idea came to her. Close by down the path, a tabby pushed his ice cream cart. Her face lit up when she glanced at Lyssa. What new mischief was in her mind now? She didn't have to wait long to hear it.

"Do you like ice cream?" She asked before standing up. Lyssa looked interested and accepted the outstretched hand from Hachi, pulling her up. Lyssa was slightly taller than the ferret although otherwise of average height. They walked down the pathway and then stopped right in front of the cart.

"How much are they?" Hachi asked him as she took out some of Michael's money from her pocket. The cat named his price, and she ordered two strawberry drumsticks. When she turned to hand Lyssa her ice cream, the fox was utterly fascinated by the treat. Lyssa almost looked like she was about to drool. Luckily, they got away before the esper could embarrass herself in front of the tabby.

"I almost forgot how these tasted," Lyssa exclaimed. "My strict diet forbids sweets like these." She hesitated for a bit until Hachi began to eat hers. At that, the fox shrugged and indulged herself.

Once she took her first bite, a syrupy, sweet flavor filled her taste buds and sent a shiver down her spine. It was refreshing and cool, and it complimented the sunny weather very well. Lyssa brought her other hand to her cheek, suppressing a moan. "If I didn't know better, I'd be thinking that you're trying to get me fat." Hachi giggled. It was interesting hearing someone who previously wasn't much more than an acquaintance and partner on a deadly mission, suddenly speaking to her so casually and affably as she now did. If circumstances were different, maybe they could live like this more.

"It's good, isn't it?" Hachi asked, nibbling her cone.

Instead of answering, the esper snatched Hachi's cone and fled. *Oh, so that was it?* Hachi thought. Time for payback. What hurt could a little more fun do? She shot after her as they veered all around the park, evading the ninja girl amidst laughter. Hachi put too much energy in the chase while Lyssa wasn't running at max speed, so she caught her before the pond as the two doubled over to catch their breath. Hachi got her ice cream back, and she could tell that the white fox was feeling better. The sun's intensity dropped then, a sign that the afternoon was winding down.

The two were already on their way out of the park and back to the safehouse. They needed to get back before supper. Michael has to be cooking something good, and Hachi definitely didn't want to be late for that. Plus, they had that tracker to check on tonight.

"Thank you for the outing, Hachi," Lyssa told the ferret.

With a wink, she held her two fingers up, spread apart in a peace sign. "No problem, you deserve it." Moments like these were important to have, even if they are short-lived—it was better than never to experience them at all.

They finished their treats as they made it to the fence. Walking up the steps, they made it back to the front door. Michael answered them shortly after they rang the bell. With one look he could tell that they had a fun time.

"Welcome back, ladies. Dinner is in the oven." Michael told them as they went to their respective rooms to get changed. Hachi raised her brow reproachfully at his statement while she passed him. By the time they were done freshening up, he had called out "The table's set and it's piping hot!"

Both ladies found their way to the kitchen in a short time, their steps boosted by good appetites. The table had already been set—a fine white cloth sat atop a long dining table set with three wide plates piled with a combination of meats and veggies. Hachi could not deny that the salaryman was a more than decent cook. With quality food like this, how could she complain?

The shinobi took her seat, and Lyssa followed suit. Her opinion of the fox had changed since they first met. The esper wasn't as cold-hearted as she first appeared. She was someone entirely different than what she'd taken from their first encounter. *I wonder if she feels the same way about me?* Hachi thought to herself. Not that it mattered, their ways would soon part once the Nooscite issue has been resolved.

They were an unlikely team to have formed up, yet it turned out that they worked well together due to their professional backgrounds. Their similar backgrounds and shared goals worked out to their favor, in Hachi's opinion. Sure, it hadn't gone as smoothly as partnering up with Junior but it's still been better than what she initially thought it would be.

Michael joined them shortly. Hachi was worried at first about the expenses he'd been taking out to support them, but found relief in the fact that Lyssa was pitching in some as well. What was most important was resolving the nooscite issue to take some pressure off of the male ferret and focus on her primary mission.

"How did you enjoy the park?" Michael asked them, taking a swig of his soda. For some reason, he was really thirsty today. Hachi grinned at him, sipping a glass of water before she spoke.

"I made her try some ice cream." Hachi smirked as Lyssa blushed, "she hasn't had any in a long time." The white fox was not responding, looking embarrassed. This gossip wasn't really helping with her image. She was normally stoic and serious, and would've liked to keep that image up as long as she could—all she wanted was to sweep this topic under the rug.

"Really? Must have been fun. The weather was nice out today too." Michael replied, seemingly oblivious of the esper's coyness, as Lyssa looked away in silence. Hachi, feeling courteous, thought to drop the conversation before her esper friend got any more uncomfortable. At the end of the day, he was their information broker. They can always chat it up whenever the fox isn't around. Such consideration was fine with the Takaro, just to be polite.

After they were done stuffing themselves, Michael proceeded to wash the dishes. Lyssa and Hachi then went their separate ways, the latter going off to train, while the former settle down and studied. The sun gradually dipped down, and the indoor lights flipped on. When Michael went to check up on his computer, he found that it had started making a beeping noise. Upon discovering this, he called the two over—the results were now in.

Michael called the ladies in. They rushed to meet him at the computer. Michael could sense their hype building. They have all been waiting for this. It was about time they get going again, although Michael doubted if either of the ladies had had enough rest. They hunched around him as he settles down to the computer. As he began speaking, he pointed a straight finger at the computer screen as it displayed something for them.

"Great news, the tracker just came in with new information," he notified them. It looked like they were back in business. Hachi looked over past Michael's shoulder to read the screen, with Lyssa on the opposite side. The salaryman's hands settled on the desk as he pulled up the data. A routing map displayed in front of them with various photo shots on the side, showing an assortment of streets and corners. In one spot blinked a tiny red dot, and the shinobi deduced that it was their ticket to the meteorite.

"Not exactly the safest place, so that you know." Michael commented as Hachi folded her arms.

"But I like danger, Mikey. It gives me a challenge." Hachi bantered. She wasn't versed with computers, unlike Lyssa, who knew better what to expect. Michael typed in a few more lines before he showed the two some pictures and notes regarding the location marked by the blinking red dot.

"The locale is deep in mob territory, you'll be facing a lot more enemies who are ruthless at that. Not to mention that both of you aren't fully patched up." Michael looked at Lyssa. The fox shook her head brashly. He knew these girls wouldn't back down. They were far too gone beyond that.

"I don't care, this is where they took the stone right?" Lyssa knew deep down, if she permitted the stone to reach the wrong hands, it would unleash a terrible menace onto the public. Her hands balled into tight fists, her claws digging into her skin. There was no way she was going to let them catch her off guard this time. No more playing around.

"Okay, so that's where we need to go to get the nooscite back, yes?" Hachi didn't want to sound inconsiderate like she was taking it lightly. She just wanted the details so that they could get started. Personally, she wanted to get a little bit more rest in. However, time was of the essence and the more they waited, the higher the risk.

CHAPTER 8

Fated Rivalry

The forecast for that evening called for rain. Clouds gathered over the metropolitan city as the sun descended to make way for the stars, hidden as they were by the rain cloud that hovered above. Hachi listened as the first droplets fell, in a light, pitter-patter against the concrete and other hard surfaces, proving the forecast right. The windowpanes were not spared, as water from the rain thudded against them.

As the sky made the earth below its drum, Hachi and Lyssa finished their preparations. Thanks to the tracker, they had the location of the shipment, so they were leaving for it as early as they could. From their information, they'd deduced that the shipment was in the possession of some low-life don. Hachi spent the most time preparing, at least as far as gear went. Meanwhile, Lyssa had little to carry—she had her psychic prowess to thank for that—and she was ready, waiting for Hachi for a good while before the ferret was done. But now, they were both ready to roll. Hachi brandished her magical sword, thankful to have it this time. and Lyssa steeled her mind for the battle inevitable to come. They had a party to crash.

Michael logged out of his workstation to see the pair off before he left. He grunted towards the shinobi, wagging his finger to get her attention. The two ferrets met each other's glances.

"Did I forget something?" She asked the tired worker.

"Yes, your fare." He handed them some more cash with a professional smile. Given his schedule, he wouldn't be able to give them a ride this time. So he referred a trusted cab driver for the evening to transport them in his stead, before wishing them good luck. As a precaution, they were going to be dropped off a fair bit away from the hideout, where they would travel the rest of the distance on foot. If anything went awry, they'd have to find a way out on their own.

Without a convenient getaway plan at hand, the two knew that they had to be successful this time. Michael had carried his weight and then some, the females had acknowledged. With nowhere to run and nobody to bail them out, their own feet were held to the fire at this point. Anything less would mean bad consequences for both of them. Lyssa's objective is securing the Nooscite while Hachi's is capturing Lockhardt once this is resolved. Simple enough on paper.

Nevertheless, the two were both acclimated to facing such danger. Despite the less than optimal events of last evening, they felt more than ready to end this once and for all. Both were chock full of rations and weapons, Hachi now had her secret weapon too, her inherited wakizashis from Torenu that she nicknamed *'Kamui'*.

"Are you feeling nervous, Lyssa?" Hachi asked as they walked along the pavement on the side of the road, towards their pick-up point. The kunoichi's ears flicked at the drizzle as she scanned for the taxi that was going to take them.

Lyssa gave Hachi a skeptical raise of her brow. "You should know by now that getting back that Nooscite is my number one priority. Nothing will stop us this time." Her stern tone made it clear to the ninja girl that she was resolute. Nodding silently, Hachi had no more questions to ask.

As they went, Hachi couldn't help but reflect over the events passed, and how everything would very soon come to a head. She tensed as she thought back to the fight with the Chemisteer, the injuries sustained, the stress it put on Lyssa, and ultimately, the state it had left the esper in. She glanced over to the white fox, wondering to herself if she was truly ready to fight once more. But it didn't really matter. The time for action was now, whether they were fully recovered or not. Still, she was glad to have helped Lyssa get better and for spending time with Lyssa at the park. It was fun. Her train of thought stopped before they could sour into worries and regrets; there is no room for negativity in her mind right now. Soon enough, they arrived at a bus stop.

The duo were about to wait by the bus stop, but right before they did that, Hachi caught the familiar scent of a certain agent. It was Deltus. His was one that she wouldn't forget for a while, Benny had gotten away from her because of him. She had made her mind that he would pay dearly for his actions. She halted abruptly as she looked around, putting her guard up. Lyssa kept her cool demeanor as the red fox revealed himself from the shadows, giving them a slight wave with his gloved hand. It seemed that he did not wish to fight them, but Hachi didn't trust him at all.

The night that they tussled, the agent had directly caused the ferret girl's setback to her objective. She wasn't about to start listening to whatever words he had to say, but then Lyssa motioned to her that, despite Hachi's qualms, she wanted to hear what he had to tell them. The white fox displayed more tolerance to Deltus's presence than the shinobi had expected. *Do these two know each other that well?* Hachi thought to herself. On second thought, that wasn't an unlikely possibility since they both worked for the government in similar fashions.

Not wanting to come across as troubled, she decided to put her faith in the white fox. After all, if anyone should attempt diplomacy here, it should be a native unlike herself. Hachi also had a small interest in seeing this conversation play out. A cautionary doubt played around the edges off her mind, keeping her hands close to the Kamui's handles.

"Girls, I want to propose a truce." Deltus looked at Hachi, who raised her brow in suspicion. She wondered why he decided to show himself then, a riddle popped in her head—wasn't he supposed to be Lockhardt's bodyguard? She thought. He saw the ferret girl cross her arms, moving her hands away from her blades, as Lyssa shook her head.

Hachi turned away from him and said, "Why should we entertain this guy? He took my target away from me and made us look like a pair of fools."

The esper sighed. Then, the red fox continued his explanation. "The situation has changed," he said plainly. The two girls both knew why. It was because the Nooscite, which he and Lyssa were after—though for differing reasons—had been intercepted by black market criminals. That turn of events put him in the exact same boat as them. Once his spiel was through, it made more sense in their best interests to help each other out.

Nonetheless, Hachi didn't want the decision to be hers as to whether or not they would take his company. Her bias on the situation was all too clear, and in all honesty, she still wanted nothing to do with him. So she said, "I will let you decide for us, Lyssa. Whether Deltus is coming along with us or not." The ferret remained distant, continuing to avert her gaze from the foxes who seemed to have reached an agreement.

"This is Don Vinnie's hideout, Hachi. I know how you feel about Deltus, but we're seriously going to need as much help as we can get." The esper told Hachi quite matter-of-factly. Her voice betrayed little emotion, and it was clear to see her mind was sharply focused on the task at hand, nothing else. Twitching her ears, the shinobi couldn't argue with that logic, so she shrugged in resignation. However, she was visibly not pleased with the arrangement. The ninja girl glared daggers at Deltus, emanating a threatening aura. This alliance was shaky, but at least it was one less conflict to worry about. Even Hachi saw—though begrudgingly—the advantages they stand to gain on this mission, from the new addition to their party. It goes without saying.

Even so, Lyssa could easily sense the enmity seeping out of Hachi, and she understood why, which made the decision somewhat difficult for herself as well. But ultimately the white fox believed that it was not the time to be picky. She had indeed worked alongside the red fox in the past before her program's termination, so this was an exception that she would allow just for this occasion. Once the nooscite was retrieved from criminal hands, it was back to the status quo.

"Grr, I guess you're right...but that doesn't mean I've forgotten about Benny." Hachi huffed in annoyance. "He's all mine when we're through. You got that fox boy?"

The agent kept his composure. Keeping Lockhardt safe was nonetheless part of his job, even if it is currently rendered moot. He sighed and chose his next words carefully. "If this goes well, then perhaps I can arrange a meeting between you and him, little ferret."

This got Hachi's attention, but the ninja still stared at him, devoid of trust. Deltus adjusted his suit before clearing his throat like a well-mannered being. "Let's go for a walk, shall we?"

"I'll take us straight to Alberto after this. No need to worry about your crude cab. I have some information to share with you Hachi, if you don't mind, Lyssa?" Deltus turned to Lyssa, and she nodded back.

Ah, those two do know each other after all. Hachi thought. Briefly weighing her options, the Takaro hesitantly agreed and followed the two out of the alley towards an area with seating. They found a small round table on a deck. Four chairs surrounded the table, of which the group took three, to seat themselves.

The place they were in was an isolated garden nestled beside various fountains and dark shrubbery. The fountains were still, but with dark streaks on the stone where water once flowed. No water ran from the fountains at this hour. Out in the distance, an abandoned gazebo stood that the trio could see. Dark clouds hinted at rain later in the evening. Hachi was beginning to think this might be a trap from Deltus to make her let her guard down. But, no matter what, she had already committed to seeing this through to the end.

The ferret hated the engulfing silence and she had no good feeling from the dead stillness of the garden. It all seemed foreboding to her, like bad things were going to happen. This unease manifested to anyone who watched her squirm uncomfortably in her seat. Who is to say that this whole deal was just a trap set by the red fox? Still, it made sense that he wanted a truce, now that the Nooscite has changed hands to a clear enemy. The complexities of this society continue to remain a mystery beyond her simple likings.

Growing bored of this silence, Hachi leaned over and asked, "So what is it?" This had better be good, she thought.

Deltus sensed her impatience. Taking a deep breath, he thought of some possible scenarios on how to earn her trust. His brown eyes, hidden behind his shades, swept over the vicinity to spot any unwanted listeners. Finding none, he looked at the ferret girl and relaxed his shoulders.

"Alright, I shall tell you more about where I come from. You see, I was a part of a government initiative just like Lyssa." This drew Hachi's interest, her ears perking up. Lyssa didn't bother to interrupt when Deltus gave a formal pause. "You may ask me to clear anything up at any time, so-" He folded his arms as he resumed, leaving that part of his speech hanging.

Hachi's opinion of him still stood. But learning more about the foxes would help her feel more comfortable when it comes to dealing with their kind. Today's ally could be tomorrow's foe. The fact that they are working together now instead of against each other like in the past wasn't very important. The present is much more valuable than the past. She could think of no questions to ask just yet, so for now, she continued to listen to his story.

"The government jumpstarted two programs, one that made agents like me and another that made espers like Lyssa. Over time, the feds favored agents over espers. Thus, the psychic branch was disposed of. Agents outnumbered espers and they were in more demand, too." Deltus glanced at Lyssa who kept her composure. He couldn't help but ponder at the esper's lack of a reaction. Normally, she wouldn't want these details to be shared, but it seemed that Hachi had earned the right to be in the loop from her, which Deltus mused was quite the feat. "My experience was valued top among my organization and Ms. Fox here was an exceptional success."

He continued on, "You can say that we are the cream of the crop. However, internal conflicts sprouted within the government while we were undertaking operations on their behalf. It didn't look out of the ordinary on the outside. But it was there, just under the radar, and nobody felt the need to stop it."

Lyssa watched the shinobi from the corner of her eye. She figured it was only a matter of time before the truth came out, but now was a better time than any other. It's not like there was anything malicious to hide about their past, especially not from someone like the Takaro. As he explained further, a faint rumbling could be heard far away. "The reason why our programs were sponsored by the government was because of the increasing growth of mercenaries to this day. Private sector companies always had this right, picking up as much as they could afford. This threatens to shift the balance of public power."

Meanwhile, Hachi was processing the red fox's words. Slowly but surely, their situation was becoming more clear to her. This also taught her more about the politics in this country, which was more intricate than back home. It almost made her feel lucky, fortunate not to be encumbered by such complicated matters, but then she wondered if this also was influenced by the Dark One. He didn't seem to have an inkling about the evil god, so she didn't hold onto that thought for long. But she did notice that he kept throwing the ferret odd glances, like he was trying to read her, as expected from a fellow professional such as him.

"One of the rare successful results of the Nooscite, Lyssa had a vested interest in preventing that meteorite from ruining other's lives." Deltus sped through this part of the story since he did not have all of the information. Lyssa had explained it more in-depth with Michael earlier who gave Hachi the gist of it. She nodded and asked him to move on. There was still more info for him to go over with her.

"As I've said, corporations are getting the jump on the feds because they basically had quality over quantity. The agent program was so rigorous that few made it but it was still more reliable than espers which had too many unknown variables in it. Naturally, there were more agents produced than espers." Deltus shifted, "So this was their way of getting caught up." Hachi stared at Deltus for a few moments. Thinking he left something out, he added. "As for the nooscite, its transport was supposed to be a well-kept secret but intel got leaked by some higher officials, and a worst case scenario is now unfolding before us."

"What about Lockhardt then?" Hachi raised an eyebrow. Deltus smiled and outstretched a hand. "I'm in charge of his safety. He technically hired me, but with the stone taken by the enemy, that is more of a priority." He was being honest. If he didn't need their help in this operation, he wouldn't be speaking with them here, to begin with. Hachi didn't seem sold since she had her own agenda which she wanted him to address.

"Relax. He's safe, the last thing I want is for his life to be in any danger." He assured her.

"Then-" The ferret's words were swiftly interrupted by him.

"He's my collateral." Deltus pushed his negotiation. "Help me get the Nooscite back from those mob families, and I'll hand him over to you for interrogations. How does that sound?"

The ninja girl tensed at his proposal. He seemed amicable enough. Their backs were pressed to the wall, and the esper appeared to have implicitly vouched for him. She didn't trust him completely, yet if she refused then she couldn't deny that they would be passing a highly skilled fighter.

At the end of the day, they were all talented individuals with goals and different skillsets. Deltus was familiar with this land's tech which was something Hachi was still getting accustomed to. Letting out a sigh, the ferret cut her losses.

"You had better swear on your life, Agent Deltus." Hachi stood up in a way that meant business. Lyssa got up, too, just to move her body around and get her blood flowing. She was glad to see that Hachi understood the situation.

"I will make sure he holds up his end of the bargain when we're through." The white fox added to reassure her partner. Time grew shorter; there were still battle strategies to go over for their approach. "At this stage, I'd be fine with destroying that space rock if need be."

"Of course," Deltus said as he pushed a button on his watch. His custom car would pick them up in a flash. Now was the time to make a plan, going in without one would simply be foolish. Hachi growled as Lyssa rested her hand on the ferret's shoulder. Two is company and three is a crowd, as they say.

"Deltus can back us up and hold his own at the same time. I'm sure you've experienced his capabilities not too long ago." Lyssa pointed out to Hachi who begrudgingly agreed. The red fox did have more muscle mass than either of them. Against regular foes, the three of them together could take on a lot more with their combined forces. The esper chimed in, "I prefer not to fight close quarters with multiple enemies, myself."

"How are we retrieving the nooscite exactly?" Hachi asked them. "If what you said is true then it's going to be a *honettsu* nest there. There will be zero room for mistakes." In a game of numbers, they were bound to get fatigue from constant fighting. Injuries would follow, and Hachi worried for Lyssa's condition. She wouldn't want her to get incapacitated again, or worse. A lot was on the line, and the odds did not favor them, unfortunately. The three of them paused for a moment as the agent's black sports car pulled up.

It was quite sleek—painted a jet black with a rather aerodynamic design to it. From the way it hugged the ground, despite her aloofness with this country's technology, Hachi could see that it has a balance that could handle high speed swerves. It was a coupé tailored for such purpose like the mission they were embarking on. Needless to say, it looked quite fast.

"Well, we'll figure it out on the way. Let's get going already." Hachi exclaimed as they made their way into the agent's rusher. Michael can rest easy for tonight as Deltus would do what he was too busy to do. It was going to be a hell of a party, that's for certain.

"Ladies first," Deltus opened the door for the two, Lyssa going in first. Hachi followed suit in the back, with the red fox taking the front wheel. The interior was as expected of such a lavish and perhaps "sports-y" exterior. Dark colors like that of the outside, though closer to gray. Silver leather clothed the seats, the seatbelts straps of a charcoal black. Other than the color, the texture of the seat was foamy, designed to pamper the rider and at the same time, provide maximum comfort for each passenger. Then at the front, where Deltus sat driving, was a something of a command panel, with all manner of knobs and buttons, all backlit with colorful lighting that cast a glow on Deltus in the darkness of the motor vehicle, with its tinted windows in an already dark and gloomy night.

The engine was all too noiseless, something to expect of such an exotic car. The cool air conditioning on a raining day amused Hachi, only that she was past the feeling of amusement. The ferret still preferred the natural gust of wind over this. Given what was coming ahead, she cast a glance at Lyssa, who looked distanced. Her face was rigidly set with sheer determination. All or nothing, as both the white fox and kunoichi herself knew.

The automobile sped off into the cloudy night. Much as she had disliked it, Hachi couldn't help but feel grateful that they now had extra hands. It wasn't perfect but the time for complaints has passed. As long as he honored their agreement, if he was going to, the ferret girl could deal with it. For Michael's sake, she dared not to fuss for the rest of the ride. Her thoughts shifted to the mission ahead. It's time to start formulating a plan, the sooner the better.

CHAPTER 9

Power Seeker

The sky had been dark since the clouds had obscured the sun at dusk. Inside Deltus's speeding car, the trio brainstormed their attack plan. They batted a few suggestions amongst themselves, having just about settled on one. They all agreed on the basics, but the final details still needed fleshing out. Hachi flipped her hair as she watched the hideout come into view from the distance. It was both something familiar looking and at the same time, a place that she had never seen before. At least, that was what her intuition was telling her.

The structure stood firmly, becoming more apparent as they got closer. Hachi was caught déjà vu, something tells her that something big was about to go down tonight. Still, she pushed the odd feeling into the back of her mind, keeping her mind to the job at hand. After going over the game plan again in her mind, the ferret felt ready.

Lyssa was still conversing with Deltus when the ferret scooted closer. They were now on a hill adjacent to the mob boss's property. Moving within the downpour of the rain was a blessing since the rain had helped them stay hidden. The bright lights on the compound allowed the group to see silhouettes of the thugs that guarded the exterior. A few more were pacing around the compound, looking out for any intruders who might try to crash the gate. With this many 'guests,' it must mean that something important was happening within. Mike was right about the nooscite being there.

The hideout was situated near a countryside canyon, which would have taken a while to reach if not for Deltus. While not as tall as Majutsushi's castle, the home had been fortified similarly. Barbed wire at the top of the fence deterred trespassers from hopping over it to get inside. Not to mention the guards plastered on the corners with rifles. The mafiosos weren't fooling around, that was for sure. From the looks of it, they really did not want any unwanted visitors. The ferret eyed the concrete building, hoping to spot an easier way to get in. One blunder could pose a risk on her life as well as her teammates.

Their plan was solid though. The weather didn't appear to be letting up anytime soon, so they planned to use that to their advantage. A row of spotlights garnered the top, scanning back and forth. They should be easy enough to slip through, provided there were no mines around, but that wouldn't suit Vinnie's style. The mob boss did have the sense to stake his base out in a remote area. Cracks around the outer pavement indicate that the architecture was fairly old. As they got to work, on exiting the car, the ferret heard Lyssa speaking to her in the light rain.

"Hachi." The fox beckoned her with a claw to where she and Deltus were squatting. He took out a few items in his hands and wanted to go over his backup tools with the ladies. The agent gave them a few objects, including small guns, which the ninja looked at with curiosity. Then, the red fox cleared his throat before he started talking.

"These will make knocking the guards out child's play. However, we only have a limited number of darts in those tranqs, so make sure each shot counts." Hachi nodded in response. She knew that killing those guards would make much more noise than simply dispatching them non-lethally. That part was straightforward, but there was one issue that still needed to be brought up, Hachi thought as she pointed to the items.

"What exactly are those anyway?" She asked him while shrugging her shoulders, "I'm more used to conventional weapons like knives and such. Do you expect me to wield such odd weaponry that I lack practice with?"

The red fox brought the explosive-like device in front of the ferret first. "This is called a flashbang. Its light is blinding so I would suggest closing your eyes when you use it. Simple enough for you, right?" He moved onto the cylinder beside it. "Each container has four knockout gas bombs. Just throw them at the target, and they'll be knocked out before you know it. However, their effective radius has a limit so be mindful of that." Then, he waved his hand toward the last tool. "This one is a prototype EMP device. We may not need it after all, but it disables electronics." Hachi looked at all the gadgets one more time before nodding to the foxes who were waiting on her. Taking a deep breath, she loaded up and followed them.

"Remember, it's best that we minimize confrontation with enemies as much as possible in there. We must also make haste... I have a bad feeling about this." The agent noted.

Meanwhile, Hachi thought that breaching the place wouldn't be too hard. They were prepared this time and were seasoned experts to boot. Resting her hands on her wakizashis, she quietly wished them all the best of luck. Deltus took a gun from his belt as they kept moving.

When the three of them got close enough, they split up as discussed. Jumping into the perimeter from the ledge, Hachi headed east of the building. Lyssa went west while Deltus went towards the south, each using darkness to stay out of sight while muffling their steps with the rain. Hachi saw five guards in front of her and subconsciously planned her attack plan. One of the guards caught a whim of her movement, but before he could turn

112

around fully, she was already hidden behind a pillar, all set. The guard dismissed the suspicion and turned to face the other way, giving the ferret the time needed to unleash the gas at them. They slumped, one after the other and Hachi pressed onward.

The foxes had their own guards, which they took care of without much fuss. Deltus didn't meet a group, so he kept his the gas for later. He waited in the shadow as a lone guard patrolled closer. When the guard was within reach, he darted out in a flash, dispatching him without any noise. Deltus proceeded and soon came behind another. Again, moving swiftly within the rain, he took him out in no time with a ruthless kick.

While this was going on, Lyssa spotted a group of three ahead. She knew what she had to, taking proper aim with the tranqs. Using her telekinetic ability, she rustled the foliage in the opposite direction. The guards turned towards the source of that noise, their backs facing the white fox. The esper took three rapid successive shots, downing them all at once. She ventured on, searching for opening like the others. None of them had found an entrance yet though. Taking the front doors was out of the question since it would blow their cover.

Hachi tossed a sleeping bomb at yet another small group, making sure to stay upwind and hide as the white gas engulfed the patrollers. They coughed before falling to the ground. *This stuff is strong*, she thought. Eventually, the gas dissipated. Moving past the snoozing guards, the ninja girl kept at her search for a door or another way inside Alberto's base.

Lyssa had opted to use her usual enhanced fighting style to control the strain on her body. The white fox skillfully slinked out of the bushes and took out a couple more of guards, making them unconscious via chokeholds before she shoved them aside. Fortunately, she had the foresight to have the group bring radios so that they could communicate while on the field, just in case. Her back settled against a cool wall - only for a stray guard nearby to panic and take a blind shot at her general direction. She cursed quietly for missing him, as the ricocheting bullet nearly hit her. Such rotten luck at a time like this.

Deltus heard the commotion and switched gears. Running to Lyssa's location, he tossed a sleeping gas capsule into a hall where minions were piling out in response to the alert risen. He had to improvise somehow, taking cover behind a pillar as he pulled out his magnum and began to fire back at hostiles. He had only fired a few shots but what he got in response was a barrage, as the goons began emptying their automatic assault weapons at him. The air soon filled with gunshots as chaos spread throughout the facility. Whenever he ran out of ammo, he picked up a fallen thug's weapon and resumed his work. It did not take too long before he was at the esper's side. They took care of each other's blind spots, both trying to figure out how to turn the tide on this situation.

"Just like old times," the red fox remarked between the flashes of their shots.

"Shut up and fight," she scoffed back in a rare show of emotion.

On Hachi's end, she was being stared down by a pair of wallaby guards. The area turned out to be on lighter watched since most of the attention was being focused where the foxes were. When the marsupials raised their guns, she reacted fast and took evasive action. It was by instinct at that point. A flurry of bullets flew by, and Hachi ran up the wall in order to avoid the gunfire. Swearing under her breath, she scrambled to get one of the flash grenades out and ready. Then, she pulled its pin and threw it as she climbed over the railing, narrowly escaping their range. She landed as the bomb exploded like her movement was in perfect synch.

The bang went off, disorienting the shinobi for a moment. Her ears twitched as she found a widely unlocked door, which likely resulted from the foxes' diversion. Hachi took her chance and entered the vacant opening, taking care to cover her front with a trusted knife.

Lyssa retreated behind cover as the shots raining down on them intensified. They had to move, since staying in one place would only make their predicament worse. If only they could secure an opening to break free and find a way indoors. It wouldn't be long until the bosses who were having their meeting inside would be notified about the intruders by their lackeys. Working together, the esper and agent fought in tandem. They made a beeline towards the less illuminated alleyways. The white fox focused her energy on defensive barriers while the red fox picked off goons who got too close with near perfect shots. To an onlooker, the vulpines made it look easy, but it was actually anything but. A few close calls really laid down the pressure, some rounds bounced in between them. More underlings were on their way, most of them carrying shotguns, one of them carrying a grenade launcher. Deltus reached at his collar in response and gave a tired sigh.

"It looks like I have no choice." He muttered.

It appeared that they were able to drive out the lighter armed thugs, but the heavy firepower ones were advancing towards them. "Zeta option activate. Coordinates X-K 35.2127°." The shaded agent fiddled with a hidden console on his person while he spoke those cryptic words. Lyssa was about to go forward with a counterattack, but Deltus stretched his arm out, blocking her way.

"What are you-?" Her complaint was interrupted by the agent.

115

"Saving our hides." With that, a bright flash burst into the courtyard. A loud, terrifying boom accompanied it. It was strong enough to overwhelm the senses of anybody who directly faced it. Even the white fox had to flinch from the shockwave that felt, unlike any lightning strike that she had experienced before. Even before the resulting smoke cleared out, the esper felt an unfamiliar silence descend around them. The smoke gradually lifted and what was left was smoked earth and dead bodies with weapons strewn across, utterly destroyed.

"Th-that was..." Lyssa spoke, totally bewildered. Drawing out the enemy's main force to the open was definitely one of her old colleague's more devious contingency plans.

"Yes, a satellite strike. A small one, mind you." The agent flippantly replied before turning away from the scene. "Now, I'll be required to file some extra paperwork once I return to headquarters after this mission."

Lyssa took a moment to psyche herself back from the spectacle. To think that the red fox held such a trump card of his own and even having the guts to use it! With the rest of the guards finished off, the two looked around and noticed that Hachi was nowhere nearby. She must have already found a way in, they deduced and the foxes doubled their efforts to catch up with her.

Hachi moved silently as her sight recovered from that odd flash outside earlier. She had seen a light slide down from the sky, like a falling star. It landed and erupted with a tremor, catching the shinobi by surprise briefly. Moving on, the ninja slithered down the corridor past some sentries before reaching a large walkway sitting above a conference room. From what she was able to see, all the mob leaders were convening below. Crouching low, she eavesdropped on them. Naturally, they were filled with dread when they received news about the attack outside. Not knowing when the other two were going to show up, Hachi decided to do recon by herself. The radio signal was weak where the shinobi was, and she didn't feel like jumping the gun just yet.

Meanwhile, Lyssa and Deltus were still searching for a way in. To speed up the process, the pair separated once again to cover more ground. That last fight took a considerable amount of the esper's mental reserves, but it was necessary. Not to mention, she still had enough to fight adequately. Lyssa snuck up behind some stragglers and struck them in the back of the necks, sending them rolling. Before either of them could move, she stuck a knife each in each of their chests. She chuckled, knowing that she picked that useful skill up from the shinobi. She glanced beside to see Deltus crashing through the door. He had found a way inside and with it, a couple of guards that stayed behind for cover. He took one out with a perfect shot and used the other as a shield to break down another door at the other end of the room. He rushed the thug fast enough to split the wooden door in half.

Deltus reloaded his gun, watching the lifeless bodies he recently disposed of in front of Lyssa. The two wasted no time. Nodding to one another, they went in deeper with caution, each watching the other's blind spots. The ninja girl should be somewhere ahead. They could only pray that she didn't start the party without them.

The amount of guards in there was surprisingly manageable, though the agent speculated that an order to withdraw their forces might be given out if the panic spreads somehow. Nonetheless, they took advantage of this opportunity to catch their breath before resuming their search for Hachi and the criminal bosses. "I just hope she's okay." Lyssa murmured.

"I'm sure she's fine. She knows her way around a battlefield, you know." He remarked.

Hachi was still in the meeting room unnoticed. She had some difficulty listening in, but it looked like they had been told that attackers have breached the compound and were coming for them. They stopped their negotiations to focus more on the current situation. Apparently, a huge explosion had also taken out a bulk of their forces. Hardly any of their henchmen were responding to their calls as the Takaro moved closer, to get to a better position. Midway, she saw a glimpse of the nooscite off to the side, through the bars. Fortunately, none of them had noticed her. They were too preoccupied with something else, for sure.

What are they planning to do with it? The ferret suspiciously eyed the purple rock. It looked exactly like how she imagined it, harmless at first but shrouded with mysteries from beyond the stars. *Those two better get here soon or else I'll have to start the party without them,* Hachi thought to herself, getting a bit impatient.

"Why aren't the guards posted doing their jobs?" Vinnie stood up growling, as the mobsters began to look at each other. Tension was growing in the air of the meeting room where they stood. Anxiety was starting to build up, and with the nooscite out in display, it was only a matter of time before one of them would attempt to screw the rest over. "Which one of you was it?" One of the bosses pointed accusingly to the others across the table. This deal was turning sour thanks to the external invaders. The nervous, hushed tones continued until another leader stood up.

"There have been some yahoos outside decimating our hired guns, didn't you hear all the shooting?" He pointed out to the others as if they didn't already know. Any semblance of consensus or order was quickly evaporating from the room, and each in turn now wanted to leave. Barring Vinnie, nobody was trying to calm this situation down.

"Nobody should know where this place is!" A different boss yelled, "You must've leaked out the information somehow. You set us up!" He stared daggers into Alberto who went wide-eyed in disbelief. Leaking information? What a stupid accusation. He had made the fortress hidden for long, serving as a safe haven for all their gang's meetings and not once had there been any complications like this, until now. The green reptile went on to scold the others, but when he raised his voice, it made matters worse. The hall had quickly filled with angry shouts and threats, each mob boss acting tough to the other. Hachi observed and had concluded that this botched negotiation session would only end in an ugly and violent fashion. Right when she was about to act without waiting for the fox duo, the Don coldly stood up. His patience had now ran out.

Suddenly, Vinnie frantically went for the syringe next to the nooscite behind him. It was filled with purple, glowing liquid just like the meteorite itself. It seemed that they had discovered how to extract the essence of the stone in order to obtain its power. Hachi eyed the lambent liquid swish around the medical device. The crocodile grinned with madness as he placed it by his skull. Another mobster spat out, "I bet it was him!"

Enough was enough. Alberto shook his head before injecting himself with the alien substance before anyone else had a chance to stop him. Hachi watched from afar with disgust as he emptied the whole thing into his nervous system. Jumping in right now wouldn't be wise.

"I wouldn't get any closer." Vinnie growled, "consider the deal OFF!" The rest of the guests were shocked. What he just did to himself had never even attempted nor tested before, yet he went on and did it. There was no telling what would happen next, the worst case spelled doom for them all. The don looked prepared to risk everything though as the liquid finished oozing into his head and the effects started to take hold immediately.

He doubled over, realizing that injecting the nooscite into himself was a grave mistake. His eyes took on an eerie glow, as his mouth began to froth uncontrollably. The don grunted and groaned with pain, clutching his head and knocking over his chair. Anthros were not meant to be imbued with this ability in such a short time, and the attempt would not pass without dire repercussions. The large reptile writhed against the table, which caused the other bosses to back away slowly. Then, Hachi felt a violent pulse ripple as the crocodile unleashed a wave of psychic energy that knocked the rest of the individuals inside the meeting room down to the floor. In other words, it sent them flying about the room before they finally hit the ground or the walls. The ferret paled at what she had just witnessed; the force shook the building like a mini-earthquake. She knew that these tremors were bad news. He had to be stopped somehow.

Alberto proceeded to strike his claws at the mob boss nearest to him to try and channel his supernatural fury. It pierced through the criminal's chest, spattering nearby surfaces with his blood as he met a short, but brutal death. What followed was more of the same. The others fought for passage towards the exit in a mad dash to escape. Those in the ground scrambled up to resume their fleeing. It was literally every man for himself. The crocodile no longer had the capacity to reason and was reduced to a raging death machine. He emitted another shockwave in agony, throwing the traitors awry and halting their escape. Ominous energy formed around him and crackled through the air, tearing the room apart. With his newly acquired telekinesis, he took hold of the criminals' bodies, along with crushed debris from the crumbling room lying all about, and shook, sending everything into rattling disarray. Between what remained of walls, ceilings, and floors, and the stray chunks of ceiling and other materials, there was no chance of survival. Soon, his business partners all laid lifelessly on the floor, many mangled unrecognizable, some torn apart or crushed outright. Hachi saw the foxes finally arrive. The ferret met them post haste, slipping by the mad beast.

"He's lost control." Hachi informed them, Lyssa looking on, mortified by the news. Deltus took a look and took an exasperated sigh. He could see that the crocodile was not done yet. The building shook once more but this time with greater intensity. Pieces of the ceiling had started to fall. This unstable crocodile with deadly powers had to be eliminated or else. The red fox considered his satellite laser, studying the mob boss from the distance who let out another shockwave that inflicted more damages to the surrounding structure around them. The end was here. *Too bad it's only effective outdoors*, he mused.

CHAPTER 10

Adieu

The group watched on as the rampaging crocodile surrounded himself with a thick psionic field, which fluctuated erratically, brimming with alien power. The building they stood in shook from the force, evidently weakened by the crocodile's earlier display of power. Hachi wondered grimly if they would even be able to escape this fight alive. Her white fox friend seemed equally distraught.

The reptilian boss's base symptoms were not unfamiliar to her, but they were on a magnitude unlike anything she had ever seen. The sheer intensity alarmed her. And to reach the nooscite, they would have to get through him. Lyssa admitted to the others that she might not be able to fight someone like this and win, even with her experience. Deltus scoffed and stubbornly fired his weapon at the mobster anyway.

It was futile. Alberto's current state rendered him immune to such attacks. With a gesture from his claw, the bullets stopped in mid-air. Then, one flick of his wrist and those same bullets came flying back at the three, forcing them to take cover. The only thing Deltus's attack did was alert Alberto to the intruders. The red fox shoved his weapon back onto its holster, clearly vexed. He didn't have any ideas, but a group effort was needed to stand a chance against this foe. Individual attacks will not work here, he silently noted.

Hachi had her own ideas. She rushed towards the don, unsheathing her wakizashis then gracefully clearing a dilapidated table that stood in her way. She was now standing back in the center of the room where the other leaders had been slain. She held her blades forward, a sigil on each of them flashing, as a fierce burst of wind shot forth towards the green beast. The ferret let forth with all her might and hoped with all her heart that the blast would pierce the raging croc.

However, Vinnie was more powerful than she had thought. Alberto let loose with a blast of his own, overpowering her attack and sending the shinobi flying backward. The esper behind her managed to slow her down with her power as the ferret's back crashed into the concrete wall, making her cough up some blood. Pain spread throughout her body but thanks to Lyssa, it wasn't fatal.

Lyssa was glad that she caught her friend in time. However, the situation still looked dire. Hachi couldn't get near him at all and Deltus's marksman skills were useless against a being that could stop bullets. How exactly were they supposed to stop him?

A shockwave snapped the three back to reality. The building's integrity rapidly decayed, and they had little time before the whole facility came crashing down on them. Support pillars all around them cracked and shuddered from Vinnie's blind rampage. His eyes were wild, glowing with a malicious violet hue. The group struggled to keep their balance as more tremors began to split the ground beneath them. The agent gathered them all together at a safe distance, barking at his teammates.

"We're not going to beat him one-on-one." He told them while Alberto clutched his head again in pain. He let out an agonizing shriek that made the group cover their ears. Hachi even felt the sound waves vibrating through her teeth. This time, however, she kept to herself. The ferret looked to the white fox to see if she had any ideas.

"Well? What should we do Lyssa?" she asked.

"You two won't be able to do anything to him," Lyssa's gaze narrowed on the intoxicated mobster. "I'll take care of him by myself." The esper answered.

Deltus was taken aback by her grim suggestion, "Lyssa...are you sure about this?"

"I wish there was another way but..." A chunk of the ceiling fell from above them, and the three narrowly sidestepped out of the way. The debris punched a hole through the walkway and burst forth a plume of dust. "I'm the only one who can contain him within these grounds." Alberto had now shifted his attention to the intruders. Just one hit was all it might take to kill any of them, so they raised their guard preemptively.

The don's madness had reached the point where speech had been robbed from him completely. He screamed, hurling another blast of psychic energy at the group. The building's crumbling and destruction was exponentially increasing. Lyssa nullified the wave around their area with her own power. It strained her mind but she was used to it, and she wasn't about to lose her partners over this. All of her missions to this point, came down to this night. Knowing what she had to do and the price she would have to pay, the esper took a deep breath to compose herself.

"You two need to run, I'll stop him," the white fox declared. She began to walk toward the livid crocodile, slowly. On seeing her approach, it snarled at her in response. Suddenly, Vinnie levitated a few heavy objects behind him and charged at Lyssa. Hachi moved to help, but Deltus quickly restrained her. He whisked the ferret to a safer distance from the psychic battle, finding cover for the two of them. Vinnie swung at Lyssa with his tail, and she jumped high into the air, his tail smashing into a wall instead. Using this opening, she used her telekinesis to pelt him with debris from above. But in no time at all, he stood back up and shook it off like it was nothing. Hachi looked back, worried for the white fox's safety and desperately wanting to help.

"Come on Hachi," Deltus urged the ferret girl to proceed. "Keep moving, before this whole place does us in." The psychic battle between Vinnie and Lyssa was too intense, too dangerous for them to try and join in, but the ferret couldn't stop thinking about how Lyssa would fare. How long could she keep him at bay? She didn't want to let Lyssa fight such a hopeless battle alone, abandoning her on a suicidal mission, not like this.

"I'm not leaving her behind!" The Takaro finally shouted, now struggling against the agent's grasp, "Get your dirty mitts off me! We can't let her do this!" Finally, she shoved the red fox to the ground before rushing back to the room where Vinnie and Lyssa still fought. When the esper noticed her return, she immediately reprimanded the ferret.

"LEAVE! This is MY responsibility, so go before I make you myself!" she yelled above the deafening sounds of the fight. The determination in her voice resonated with Hachi deeply. The assassin didn't know where or when she had grown these sentiments for the esper—she wasn't even conscious of them until now—but now she realized they were obstructing her from fulfilling her own mission, and she would just have to overcome them. Hachi choked in her sorrow, turning back to where Deltus headed. Not only did she feel so weak, she wouldn't even have a proper chance to say goodbye.

With Hachi taken care of, Lyssa could turn her focus back to the battle, where she barely dodged another strike from the crazed mobster. The white fox retaliated with a fan kick, an attack that doubled as a way to make some distance between them. As they fought, the clock continued to tick down, with more and more of the building cracking and crumbling all around them. Lyssa attempted to suspend the reptile in midair with her psionics. She was able to penetrate his field with her focus, but he was already fighting back. All she was doing was trying to restrain him until the facility fell on top of everything. A simple plan, yet the only effective one she could think of at the moment. Her purple eyes glowed brilliantly, matching his. She was never going to back down. The crystal on her head shone as she pushed her powers to their absolute limits.

Lyssa's body was marked with cuts and bruises from her ongoing altercation with Vinnie. Her injuries were just beginning to tax on her, but the mob boss still looked totally unshaken. The esper wasn't able to keep the crocodile in check, and she blocked another wave of energy from him as he broke free of her levitation pin. She knew she was in trouble, but if she was going down, Vinnie was going down with her, that was for sure.

With the time Lyssa afforded them, Deltus was picking off any stragglers, already running toward the exit on his own. In the back of his mind, he was hoping that Lyssa could convince Hachi to back down, hoping that the Takaro would be joining him soon. He didn't know it yet, but Hachi was already sprinting after him, running past bodies left in his wake. She has yet to see him yet, but she knew she was close when she heard the red fox cry out. When she had caught up, a thick slab of cement had pinned his leg down.

"Deltus..." Hachi stopped to help him, but the building was at best, a minute or two from imploding.

"GO! Don't concern yourself over me!" He commanded her. It was something she didn't expect him to say to her at all. The ninja turned away, gritting her teeth.

128

As he was vainly trying to free himself, Hachi made it out of the building. She didn't stop running until she was near the exterior walls and clear from any falling objects. The surrounding area was barren, cool from the clouds rolling in. It was still dark outside, but the rain had since stopped. Her eyes strained to see the building give way and collapse in on itself. Despite her hopes, it was certain that the others didn't make it in time.

Most of the exterior had been reduced to rubble, dust billowing up into the sky as the tremors finally subsided. She couldn't believe they were gone, just like that. Her heart sank, and she gave a solemn bow to her lost allies. She'd take only a moment of mourning, though, before the fatigue and pain from her injuries came over her in full force. That's when she realized she barely had the strength left even to stay standing.

Following the aftermath, came silence. By now, all goons outside of the building had vanished. Likely fled the scene after they witnessed the calamity happening inside. At that site, she was all that remained. The Takaro took comfort that at least the nooscite was no longer a threat to the world. Hachi bit her lip, her hand squeezing tightly onto the handle of her blade for comfort. It seemed her emotions had gotten the better of her just this once. She shed a few tears that she quickly wiped away. After a couple of minutes, Hachi heard somebody behind her.

"Who are you!?" Hachi spun around, ready to fight this newcomer. It was a well-dressed fennec fox. He wore a black suit and tie, much like Deltus did along with a pair of dark shades over his eyes. The vulpine was calm and tactful as his peer. Naturally, his demeanor was something that bothered her. She didn't know he had a partner or why he'd shown up after all was done. Perhaps he was there to clean up any loose ends...She kept her wits about, in any case.

"Take it easy, Miss Hachi. I'm simply a messenger of Deltus." The fennec looked at the fallen building. It was nothing but a pile of cement and metal now. "Is that-?" Hachi sighed and nodded back to the messenger. "I see...He requested I bring you to Lockhardt now that this ordeal has been taken care of."

"Deltus got trapped inside...I don't think he or Lyssa made it." The agent didn't reach out for more info, as far as she could tell. However, he was there for a different reason. Extending his hand to Hachi, it was about time she got her end of the bargain anyway. Benny was still out there, and there was still work to do for the sake of her own mission.

"By the by, you may call me Kaplan." He curtly introduced himself to the ferret while they left the destroyed compound.

The red fox's associate took Hachi by car to where the hyena brother was being held. It was near the city but not quite. Either way, it was an ingenious location to hold her target. Since he had eluded her that night, she had wanted to get her hands on him for intel he has on the Dark One. There was a chance that the agent was luring her to a trap, but she was willing to take that risk. Holding Deltus to his last words was the least she could do, she thought as she clenched her fists in anticipation.

Nearly an hour later, they arrived in front of a large white building. Hachi got out of the vehicle promptly, taking the sights in carefully. The agent politely led the way for her so that she wouldn't wander off. Past the large glass doors and down the hallway, the shinobi was brought to the basement area where the secure living space wing was. It was like private quarters except shaped like a prison block. Inside, the hyena that she had been after was watching TV. She stepped inside his room after Kaplan opened the door and left her alone. Cracking her knuckles, the ferret went to face the weapons dealer straight on.

130

Her arrival had knocked Lockhardt out of his reverie. The hyena was baffled at how Hachi managed to get inside his room. For her to locate and reach him should have been impossible. He was utterly shocked, and she did not appear to be interested in beating around the bush. "Well now, long time no see Benny." She began rather coldly.

"W-w-what are you d-doing here? W-where's Deltus!?" He was frozen in fear, unable to look the ferret in the eye. Hachi found his muttering voice annoying. The ninja girl slammed a fist on the table before she sat down in front of him, staring him down. As expected, he got intimidated fast. It took all he had not to be reduced to a nervous, quivering wreck.

"He's dead. I'm here for answers that you know, brother of Tekiya! So be a good boy and give…them…to…me!" Hachi glided her kunai across the contours of his body, close to his skin. Close enough to cut or draw blood anytime she wanted to.

Deltus is dead? He hoped that this was all a bluff, but even so, the reality was staring at his face like daggers. There is no way that this was a mere trick. She had dried blood on her body, and to the hyena, it reeked. Lockhardt felt like he couldn't last much longer to have someone with such killing intent be this close to him.

"Oh, I would cooperate if I were you." The fennec agent broadcasted his voice over a speaker inside the hyena's room. He was watching them somehow. Benny had become paranoid. He had hired this organization to protect him, but now they are stabbing him on the back like this. Hachi was losing her patience and turned her blade to apply some pressure. The hyena cried as he was getting dangerously close to becoming flayed.

"I swear, I will show you a new meaning of torture if you don't give me what I want, Lockhardt!" Hachi gave him an ultimatum, whether or not she was allowed to do such a thing barely mattered. For her, this was personal. And it was also for the greater good. Seeing no other choice, the arms dealer swallowed and gave in, shaking in his socks.

"Alright...g-give me something to write on..." Lockhardt requested. Hachi looked around and handed the hyena a notepad and pen. She briefly explained her chat with his deceased brother to him and wrung him out for leads. As he got to work, she leaned back in her chair, crossing her arms as she carefully watched his movements. He might not have been directly involved with the Dark One, but he was still indubitably an accomplice to somebody who did. Questions were exchanged back and forth, words got scrawled onto the pages. Names, dates, and other information were compiled into a list that made the ferret's tail twitch with interest.

Things were finally looking up for Hachi this evening—no, morning. With this new list of leads, she now has specific targets to go after with addresses to boot. Once he finished scribbling items down, he shoved the notes to the shinobi. The ferret skimmed through them for any problems, until she was satisfied that it was all good.

"Perfect." A grin marked her face as she stowed away the documents. Benny breathed uneasily, hoping that she would leave him be now. He was never a big fan of pain, so he humbly requested her to take her leave. Of course, he wouldn't feel completely safe until she got out of the room and his sight. The way it should be.

"Are we good now? Will you leave me alone from this point on?"

"Hmph, you better hope you're not hiding anything from me. Because I will have these papers thoroughly cross-examined."

Hachi warned him before turning towards the exit. Exiting back upstairs into the main lobby, Kaplan approached her to see how well she was satisfied. She told the fennec that she needed to share these notes with her other partner as soon as possible, so that they could verify and analyze it. From there, they could plan their next move. The agent stopped her for a moment and spoke in a matter-of-fact tone.

"I know it doesn't mean much coming from me, but I want to personally thank you on behalf of the agency of Pennotia for helping us resolve the nooscite problem. I do hope you find what you're looking for from that person, Miss Hachi." Hachi blinked, not expecting that thanks from him. Nonetheless, she bowed her head, politely accepting it.

"I hope so too, to be honest." She really wanted to get to the bottom of the matter regarding this Dark One as well. "Perhaps, we'll keep in touch?"

"A proposal worth considering, no doubt," the vulpine leaned back in reply.

Like she said, first she had to confirm the information at Michael's place. Kaplan assured Hachi that Lockhardt would remain in custody until she double-checked the data that she obtained from the hyena. This way, she wouldn't have to hunt him down again which would be a major pain for her. The ninja didn't worry too much though, since Lockhardt didn't have much of a spine when she met him, but it was better safe than sorry. Experience taught her that. She doesn't know what they were going to do with the deceased foxes' bodies and Benny's fate once she moves ahead. She doubted if they would actually release him at all.

In any case, it wasn't her business to pry in. With their deal concluded, she left the agents' base to return back to Mike's where he could review the material from those notes. Of course, she took a long, well-deserved nap that day.

Epilogue

To my dear friend Takaro,

I was most glad when I had received your letter, Hachi. It sounds like your time in Pennotia so far had been beneficial. To answer your question, things are going well here. Remember our mentor, Torenu? That old Mastiff is still training new warriors even as I dip my ink. He wishes to bid you good fortune on your quest. May his teachings help guide you while you're on the field. Back to me though. I am still grasping how it is to be a leader. It is not as easy as it sounds. I now have other people to worry about, along with my own well-being, which I must watch in order to ensure that I fulfill my duties. There are a lot of lessons to learn and thanks to the support from the clan council and our friends; I am on the path to understanding true leadership.

I may not be as charismatic in general as my father, but I do try my best. As a fellow shinobi, it takes an effort to speak to groups instead of relying solely on my actions. Actions may speak louder, but Torenu told me how important it is to put people's spirits at ease by giving them some peace of mind with diplomacy. I cannot show weakness nor any hostility which is what making new allies out of neighboring regional families require.

I would advise you not to overwork yourself. Remember to take breaks now and then. We've been taught meditation techniques for this very purpose as our minds are just as important as our bodies. We must be of a clear mind to do our jobs as best we can. Well, I don't want to turn this into a written lecture so I'll move on. You are an exemplary ninja after all.

Honestly, I'm kind of jealous that you get to see new places and experience new things while I languish here out of obligation. I have decided to somehow meet up with you at some point as soon as possible, if only just to visit briefly. As clan leader, there must be away... Anyway, is everything really how you say it is over there? I find it strange how so many people can live with such a lifestyle. Then again, they would probably say the same thing about us with our rural way of life, so it balances out.

The dark one poses a formidable threat indeed, but I know that you can do it; I believe in your skills. Don't be afraid to get new gear when the situation calls for it. You can be stubborn at times; I know because I'm the same way. Though, you should always carry some sort of concealed weapon on you. Our lives are key to accomplishing our goals.

I have some very important news to share with you. One of our scouts in the Shimada province had spotted a ferret in custody who matched the description of your mother. If his report is correct, then she is still alive but has been captured and kept under strict watch. I tried to get more information out of him, but that was all we could learn for now. It's frustrating because as soon as I heard about it, I wanted to form a rescue party, but I find myself too busy to take action immediately, so I apologize.

Your mother being seen was quite the stroke of luck for us, and know that I will dedicate our resources in getting her back safely. We will also expand our networks in and around the Shimada province to better aid us in our efforts. This, I promise you Hachi, and please know that I never break my promises.

With that out of the way, do not let this distract you from your primary task. For the time being, I am preoccupied with politics, and I must have them see in me a worthy leader to move forward. But what am I saying? It was a nice break to be able to sit down and exchange letters with you like this. Reading yours was definitely interesting. May we continue to communicate this way as often as we have the luxury to.

It's nice that your acquaintance Mike has helped you adjust in your journey. He sounds reliable; it must be tough for him to accommodate you as best as he did—even though it was because you dragged him into it. The stars are quite beautiful here at night. They won't be going anywhere any time soon so they will be waiting for you whenever you return.

I shall reiterate that I plan on joining you overseas once matters here have been taken care of. Whether you want to participate in Izumi's rescue operation or not is up to you. You know what they say, the more things change, the more they stay the same. I've got enough reason to go after the Dark One myself. I do hope that you don't find it imposing, but I can hardly wait to fight by your side again as comrades. Then, we can tell each other more tales about our battles and accomplishments since we last met.

Best Regards,

Junior Hitoshi

[END]

Afterword

Hello again fellow readers, this is Paradox-F. It looks like I have to type some more words so here I go.

It took longer than expected, by several months, but the physical version of my first novella's sequel is now out and about. As always, it is satisfying to share more of this world with you all. Please don't forget to check out my webcomic site Crossing-Over (**www.co-comic.com**) to read the main series where this side story came from. Also, kindly support our Patreon if you like. Every bit makes a difference. Like I mentioned in the digital edition released a bit earlier, I'm considering a third book down the road. Keep a look out for any future announcements from us about it. This sequel light novel started around the end of 2016. I shall continue to create stories that I love and promote them to other folks. Of course, I want to thank my teammates for helping this book get made. And the wonderful readers, who watch my characters come to life and do cool things, thank you all. Alright, back to working on my webcomic. Until next time, take care.

Have an awesome day!

P.S. : I've put QR codes of the book's art on here so feel free to scan and enjoy them!

Character Art

HACHI TAKARO

Name: Hachi Takaro Age: 16 Height: 163cm Weight: 61kg

The sole survivor of the Takaro clan being wiped out in her younger days. She traveled from her homeland Nihon to Pennotia to take down the Dark One who was the source of her family and land's strife. Despite being exceptionally talented in combat arts and the like, this ferret ninja is still learning to adjust to norms and cultures outside of her own.

ESPER LYSSA

Name: Lyssa Hendricks Age: 19 Height: 165cm Weight: 58kg

One of the first, and best, operatives made from the now defunct, clandestine Esper program. She has a deep sense of duty and drive to complete the mission at any cost, much like a loyal soldier. Due to a period of isolation, she appears cold and aloof but underneath that veneer lies a good person. Extensive training has given this white fox a formidable mastery in regards to her psychic powers.

AGENT DELTUS

Real Name: Reginald Stephen Age: 21 Height: 181cm Weight: 77kg

An elite agent from the federal government's Agent initiative where he received his special training from. This red fox plans his moves ahead in detail and utilizes tech to 'keep up' with the competition. He has had some history with Lyssa at some point but not much is known past that. Often underestimated, countless foes regret making that mistake after facing him.

CHEMISTEER

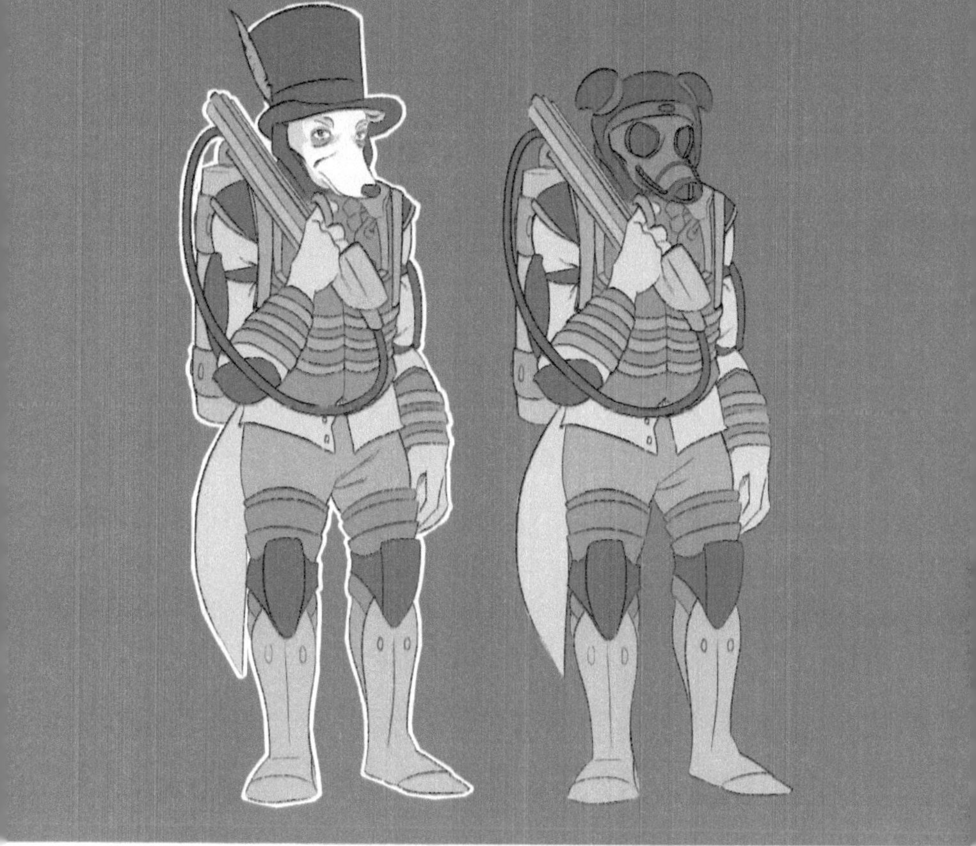

Real Name: Sebastian Felipe Age: 74 Height: 172cm Weight: 72kg

An enigmatic being who is actually a veteran mercenary that favors chemical weaponry and poisons. The origin of this possum is unclear but his experience and savvy towards toxins are a force to be reckoned with. Most profiteers at his age would have already retired but somehow he continues working well past his prime. His peculiar equipment appears to be from another era or place like Hachi was.

"DON" VINNIE ALBERTO

Name: Vincent Alberto Age: 45 Height: 188cm Weight: 84kg

A middle-aged crocodile mob boss who deals in criminal activities with other gangster families of the city such as drug smuggling and illegal trafficking. Being in business for years, he regularly escapes justice thanks to the vast connections he controls within his underground network. Lately, he has been expanding his operations boldly until rumors of a certain fabled meteorite caught his attention…

www.ingramcontent.com/pod-product-compliance
Lightning Source LLC
Chambersburg PA
CBHW020650180626
46816CB00003B/1217